Book 1 in the Family, Friends and Forgiveness Series
(originally The Children's Material)

Little Lamb's
BIG BOOK

Little Lamb—The Miracle Fables

The Children's Workbook of Daily Lessons

Cut and Color Projects

Instructions for Working with Children

Spanish Translation of Fables and Workbook

Written and illustrated by

Bette Jean Cundiff

2009 Revised with Spanish translation

ISBN 1452890854

LCCN 2010907704

Published by Miracle Experiences and You
Oracle, Arizona

THE FAMILY, FRIENDS AND FORGIVENESS SERIES

by Bette Jean Cundiff

Originally* The Children's Material, *now revised as two books designed to be age appropriate. . .

To order these and other books go to the eStore number listed under each book.

(Book 1) Ages 3-8

Little Lamb's Big Book

A Miracle Course for the young child

***With spanish translation of fables and lessons**

The beloved Little Lamb fables with large illustrations, one year of daily lessons, instructions for adults working with children and now coloring book pages for fun interaction.

To order Little Lamb's BIG BOOK go to: w.w.w.createspace.com/10003456634

(Book 2) Ages 8-12

Help is on the Way!

A Miracle Course for pre-teens

***With Spanish translation**

Fighting at school, bad grades, a whiny kid sister, Jerry is in despair until Will, an older teen, shares his miraculous lessons on handling life's challenges. This fun, insightful novel includes a workbook within the story, and is part of the complete "The Children's Material", recognized internationally since 1977 as a children's version of A Course in Miracles.

To order Help is On the Way! Go to: w.w.w.createspace.com/1000246404

More books in the
Family, Friends and Forgiveness Series
by Bette Jean Cundiff

To order these books: Go to the eStore number listed under each title

For children

Pack Rat's Christmas Surprise
A read aloud holiday story
With Spanish Translation
To order go to: w.w.w.createspace.com/1000238024

Mystery at the Everything Exchange
A fun mystery for young teens
To order go to: w.w.w.createspace.com/1000237835

For Adults

Side by Side—The Twelve Steps and A Course in Miracles
(with J.R. Richmond)
With Spanish Translation
To order go to: w.w.w.createspace.com/1000248448

Hand in Hand—Recovery and Miracles
From 20 years of lectures the author made on
The Twelve Steps and A Course in Miracles
To order go to: w.w.w.createspace.com/1000248396

Coming soon. . .
SOUL PROGRESSION
A complete system of study blending the ancient and modern
(Available in 2011)

You can email the author at:
bette@bettejeancundiff.com

Little Lamb

The Miracle Fables

Our Father's World

God's world was everywhere and everything. God's world was filled with love and beauty.

God's world was filled with the music of happiness. The bubbling brooks laughed happily. The sunlight danced and flickered. The trees rustled their contentment. Little Lamb was at peace in his Father's world. Here was warm sunlight, cool water to drink and green grass to eat. Here all the animals lived in love and brotherhood. Their Father was in them and around them. He spoke to them in their hearts.

One day God called to Little Lamb, "Little Lamb, I need your help."

"Yes, Father," answered Little Lamb, "How can I help you?"

And his Father said, "Little Lamb, you are perfect and loving just as all My children are. And when My children are awake in My world they can see their perfection for I love all My children and have created them this way. But sometimes My children sleep. And when they sleep they dream and in their dreams they forget My love. They forget they are perfect. They forget their Father Who is with them always and Who loves them.

"You, Little Lamb, understand this and can see the love in all your brothers and sisters. Now you must sleep and dream too. Dream Little Lamb, but in your dreams remember Me. And help your brothers and sisters to remember Me also. Teach them that the world they think they see is but a dream. Help them awaken and open their eyes to My real world for here is love and happiness."

And Little Lamb was filled with the wonder and peace of God's love.

"Yes, Father. I will sleep and I will dream. But I will remember that You are with me always. I will go into the dream world and help all my brothers and sisters to remember You and awake into Your real world."

As the sun gently dipped below the trees Little Lamb curled into a comfortable ball. The music of the birds and insects softly sang a lullaby to soothe Little Lamb to sleep. And in his heart he heard his Father's words, "You are My Son in whom I am well pleased. Your work has begun. Dream sweet dreams, Little Lamb. And in your dreams awaken My children so they may remember My love for them."

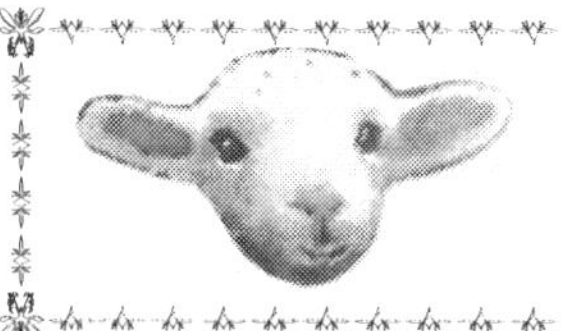

From Fear to Love

Little Lamb opened his eyes slowly. Carefully he climbed to his feet. "Learn, enjoy and teach. There is much for you to do," came God's Voice in his heart.

"Quickly, come quickly Little Lamb. We need your help." Within the dream Little Lamb opened his eyes. Around him were the animals of the forest. Mouse was scurrying here and there. Raccoon moved out of sight behind a tree stump.

"You must help us Little Lamb," said Mouse. Fear kept twitching his whiskers. "There is something awful in the forest and you must save us."

Raccoon moved further behind the tree stump hoping no one would see him.

"Have you looked to see what it is?" asked Little Lamb. "The fear in your hearts will go away when you know what it is you fear."

Mouse looked at Raccoon and twitched his whiskers angrily. Raccoon slunk further behind the stump.

"We are too afraid to look."

Little Lamb's heart went out to his friends. He knew he must discover what hid in the darkness of the forest for fear disappears in the light of love. And so off he went, fearless in his Father's love.

As darkness began to fall, Little Lamb walked deeper into the forest. His friends were far behind him. Deeper and deeper he went. The blackness covered him and he felt alone. He had forgotten his Father would be with him always.

Separated from his friends in a part of the forest he did not know, Little Lamb became afraid. The snap of a branch near him made Little Lamb jump with fright. Now he seemed to be surrounded by rustling and crackling. Little Lamb's heart pounded in his chest.

"Oh why am I here?"

And as quickly as he had asked the question, the answer came. Softly and gently the words rose from his heart.

"You are in the dream world Little Lamb and you came to help your brothers and sisters awaken because you love them as I love you."

Then Little Lamb knew he was not alone, for his Father was within him. Fear left Little Lamb, and in its place came peace and happiness for he could feel his Father's love.

For the first time Little Lamb looked up and saw the moon shining through the trees. So brightly did it shine that he could see around him as if it were day. And there, hiding behind a large bush, was an animal.

His coat was golden yellow. A large mane of fur circled his face.

It was a lion.

"Hello Lion," called Little Lamb.

As he spoke he noticed tears falling from Lion's eyes.

Gently Little Lamb asked, "Can I help you?"

"I am so lonely and frightened. Each time I come near anyone to say 'hello', they run away."

Little Lamb smiled. So this was what Mouse and Raccoon feared. It was only Lion, lonely and frightened just as they were.

"Come, do not be afraid. Let us be friends and through me you will meet the friends for whom you search."

As Little Lamb and Lion came out of the woods intothe clearing, Mouse, whiskers twitching, ran behind a boulder. Raccoon scurried under a fern, eyes large and frightened.

"Come. Don't be afraid," called Little Lamb to his friends.

"Lion was alone in the forest and needs our friendship as much as we need his. Come and meet what frightened you. For he is the same as you. Lonely and frightened he reaches out for your friendship. Can you say 'no' to him?"

And so Mouse and Raccoon slowly came forward. As the animals' fear began to disappear, friendship and love took its place.

Little Lamb could hear his Father's Voice speak to all of them in their hearts.

"Today you chose love instead of fear. For without fear, there could only be love."

Mouse said, "Thank you Little Lamb for teaching us to look through fear to the love that is always there, waiting for us to reach out and accept it."

With that Mouse reached out his hand and took Lion's paw. Fear had disappeared and only love remained in all of them. ♡

We are All Our Father's Children

Little Lamb was in the dream world. He was with all the animals of the forest. The warm evening breezes touched them gently as they sat and listened to Little Lamb speak.

Miss Rabbit moved forward shyly, and quietly asked Little Lamb, "You tell us that we are all brothers and sisters. But I don't understand. I have long ears, a fuzzy body and strong legs to hop with. Mr. and Mrs. Swan have long necks, feathers, wings to fly with and webbed feet to swim with. How can we be sisters and brothers?"

Then Owl spoke up, "Yes, Little Lamb, how can I be a brother to Miss Deer? I sleep all day and am awake all night, and she sleeps all night and is awake all day."

Bear spoke loudly in his deep voice, "Look at how big I am and how small Mouse is. How could we be brothers?"

Little Lamb smiled lovingly at his friends and said to Miss Rabbit, "What do your mother and father look like?"

And Miss Rabbit said, "Why they have long ears, a fuzzy body and strong legs just like me."

"Tell me Owl," asked Little Lamb, "What are your parents like?"

And Owl thought for a moment and said, "You know, they sleep all day and are awake all night, just like me."

Then Little Lamb turned to Bear and said, "Your father must be big, just like you."

And Bear nodded his head to answer "Yes."

"You are all your parents' children. You look like them and you act like them. Now tell me who is the Father of everyone and everything?"

And all the animals smiled and said together, "God is the Father of everyone and everything."

"Now tell me what God our Father is like."

Bear said loudly, "He is all powerful."

Owl said thoughtfully, "He is very wise and knows everything."

Miss Rabbit blushed and quietly said, "He is our Father and loves us."

Little Lamb asked his friends, "Can you see God our Father?"

And Miss Deer looked up and said, "God is in our hearts. He isn't something you see, God is love and that is something you can only feel."

Now Little Lamb looked at all his friends and said, "God our Father is powerful, and wise and loving. And He is always in our hearts ready to help us. Now think for a moment. You are your parents' children and as your parents are, so are you also. If God is in all of your hearts, then you must be in all of your brothers' and sisters' hearts also. If God is always ready to help us and love us, then we are always ready to help and love each other. For God is our Father and we are like Him."

Owl's eyes lit up and he said, "Now I understand. Our bodies are just costumes we put on for fun. They help us do our jobs. But it is what's inside that is real. That is where God is. And where God our Father is, so our brothers and sisters are also. They are in our hearts always."

Little Lamb smiled and all the animals smiled at each other. In their hearts they could hear their Father's Voice saying, "'You are all My children: powerful, wise and always loving for I have made you so."

And as the soft moonlight shone on all of them, they knew Who their Father was.

They could feel in their hearts that they were truly brothers and sisters.

They were one.

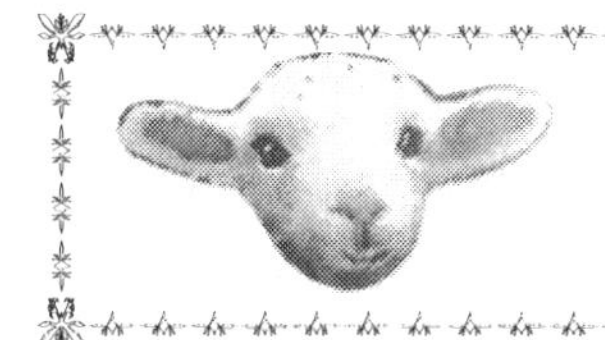

Our Father's Voice

Little Lamb remembered his Father's words. He would go deep within the dream world and awaken all those who were asleep and had forgotten their Father's world.

Darkness, as soft as a blanket, covered Little Lamb and in his sleep he began to dream. And in the dream he was on a path in a forest.

Gray Squirrel was scampering back and forth under a large tree, its leaves a bright orange.

"Hello Gray Squirrel. How are you this fine day?" asked Little Lamb.

"Terrible, terrible. That's how I am this fine Fall day. Soon the frost will be coming and then the snow. The snow will cover all the nuts and seeds and pollynoses. What shall I eat then? Oh dear, what shall I do?" And off the squirrel ran.

Little Lamb walked further down the path in the forest and there he met Bear. "Hello Bear. How are you this fine day?" asked Little Lamb.

Bear looked down sadly at Little Lamb and sighed. "The long winter is coming and I am a big bear. I am always hungry. How will I be able to live through the winter when the snow comes and the bees stop making honey for me to eat?"

Bear walked slowly into the woods sighing deeply to himself. Again Little Lamb walked further down the path. Over his head flew a flock of geese, their wings flapping loudly.

"Where are you going on such a fine day?" asked Little Lamb.

"Where, oh where, can we go?" asked the largest goose. "Soon the winter will come and the lakes will freeze and the trees will be covered with snow. Where will we live without freezing?"

And off the geese flew squawking unhappily.

Little Lamb sat down on the side of the path. He was troubled by his friends' problems. He knew he must help them, but how? And so, Little Lamb closed his eyes and within his heart he asked his Father for help.

"Father, my friends are worried and frightened." Little Lamb prayed. "They need Your help. What can I do?"

And through the mist of the dream his Father's Voice answered him.

"Tell your friends, Little Lamb, that I will listen to their questions and answer them. All they must do is ask and then listen for My answer within their hearts. I love all My children and I am always here to help them."

And so Little lamb called all the animals together and told them, "Our Father, Who is always with us will help you. All you must do is close your eyes, ask for His help and listen to your hearts. He will answer."

Gray Squirrel closed his eyes and said, "Father, I am worried. Soon the snow will cover all the nuts and seeds. How will I eat?" And then Gray Squirrel sat quietly and listened to his heart.

"Do not worry Squirrel," came his Father's Voice. "Go and gather up all the nuts and seeds you can find. Store them in the ground. Then when the winter comes you can dig them up. This way you will never be hungry."

"Thank you Father. Now I know just what to do."

And off scampered Gray Squirrel eager and happy to collect food for the winter. Bear closed his eyes and said, "Father, I am a big bear and am always hungry. I will starve this winter when the bees stop making honey. What shall I do?"

And Bear sat quietly and listened to his heart.

"Do not worry Bear," came his Father's Voice, "Follow the bees and go to the honeycomb now and eat and eat. Grow very fat Bear, and then when you sleep all winter your food will be stored in your body and you will not be hungry."

"Thank you Father. Now I know just what to do."

And off Bear went to eat honey and grow fat.

The largest goose closed his eyes and said, "Father, I must take care of my flock of geese. Where can we go when the lakes are frozen and the trees are full of snow?"

And Goose sat quietly and listened to his heart.

"Do not worry Goose," came his Father's Voice. "Take your flock and fly far to the south. There it will stay warm all winter and there you will find lakes to swim on and leafy branches to sit under."

"Thank you Father. Now I know just what to do." And off flew the flock of geese toward the South.

Little Lamb smiled. He had helped his friends. Now they knew they must only ask and then listen for their Father's loving Voice. For in their Father's love was the answer to all their questions. ♡

We Are All Our Father's Children

Little Lamb was in the dream world. He was with all the animals of the forest. The warm evening breezes touched them gently as they sat and listened to Little Lamb speak.

Miss Rabbit moved forward shyly, and quietly asked Little Lamb, "You tell us that we are all brothers and sisters. But I don't understand. I have long ears, a fuzzy body and strong legs to hop with. Mr. and Mrs.
Swan have long necks, feathers, wings to fly with and webbed feet to swim with. How can we be sisters and brothers?"

Then Owl spoke up, "Yes, Little Lamb, how can I be a brother to Miss Deer? I sleep all day and am awake all night, and she sleeps all night and is awake all day."

Bear spoke loudly in his deep voice, "Look at how big I am and how small Mouse is. How could we be brothers?"

Little Lamb smiled lovingly at his friends and said to Miss Rabbit "What do your mother and father look like?"

And Miss Rabbit said, "Why they have long ears, a fuzzy body and strong legs just like me."

"Tell me Owl," asked Little Lamb, "What are your parents like?"

And Owl thought for a moment and said, "You know, they sleep all day and are awake all night, just like me."

Then Little Lamb turned to Bear and said, "Your father must be big, just like you." And Bear nodded his head to answer "Yes."

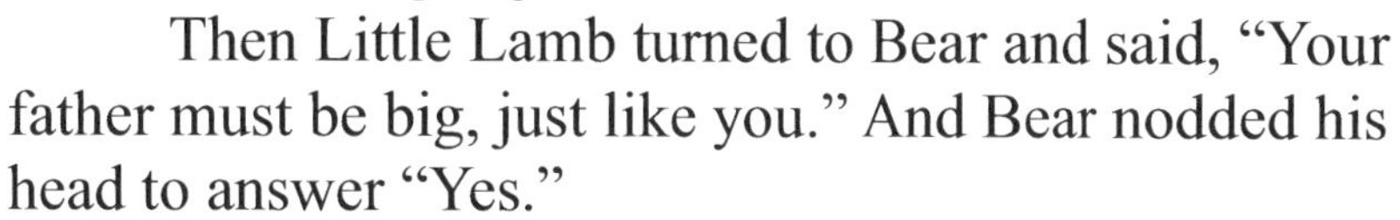

"You are all your parents' children. You look like them and you act like them. Now tell me who is the Father of everyone and everything?"

And all the animals smiled and said together, "God is the Father of everyone and everything."

"Now tell me what God our Father is like."

Bear said loudly, "He is all powerful."

Owl said thoughtfully, "He is very wise and knows everything."

Miss Rabbit blushed and quietly said, "He is our Father and loves us."

Little Lamb asked his friends, "Can you see God our Father?"

And Miss Deer looked up and said, "God is in our hearts. He isn't something you see, God is love and that is something you can only feel."

Now Little Lamb looked at all his friends and said, "God our Father is powerful, and wise and loving. And He is always in our hearts ready to help us. Now think for a moment. You are your parents' children and as your parents are, so are you also. If God is in all of your hearts, then you must be in all of your brothers' and sisters' hearts also. If God is always ready to help us and love us, then we are always ready to help and love each other. For God is our Father and we are like Him."

Owl's eyes lit up and he said, "Now I understand. Our bodies are just costumes we put on for fun. They help us do our jobs. But it is what's inside that is real. That is where God is. And where God our Father is, so our brothers and sisters are also. They are in our hearts always."

Little Lamb smiled and all the animals smiled at each other. In their hearts they could hear their Father's Voice saying, "'You are all My children: powerful, wise and always loving for I have made you so."

And as the soft moonlight shone on all of them, they could feel in their hearts that they were truly brothers and sisters.

They were one.

Forgiveness

Little Lamb closed his eyes and quickly fell asleep. He must enter the dream again for there was more work for him to do.

Two chipmunks were making a horrible noise in the grassy clearing. Both the chipmunks were chattering in anger. Bits of grass began to fly as the two began to nip and scratch each other.

"You always find the biggest nuts and never let me have any," screeched Little Chipmunk.

"That's right," yelled back the other. "Whenever I find any nuts you steal them away for yourself." And back to fighting they went. Bits of fur and grass flying into the air.

Little Lamb walked into the clearing. "My brothers, what could be making you so angry?"

Big Chipmunk stopped nipping Little Chipmunk and said, "Every day I get up very early and work hard gathering nuts to eat. And every night when I am fast asleep he comes and steals them. This is not fair."

Little Chipmunk looked up at Little Lamb, tears of hurt and anger in his eyes. "Big Chipmunk never shares his nuts with me. Every day we go out to search for nuts to eat. And every day he finds the biggest and the most. I am much smaller than he is. I cannot run as fast so I cannot find them first. I am not as strong so I cannot carry as many as he can. I am always hungry and never have enough to eat. While he always has more than enough to eat. This is not fair. So when Big Chipmunk is not looking I steal some of his nuts for myself."

Little Lamb looked at both the chipmunks. He could see the fear each of them had in his heart. He could see that it was this fear that was making them angry with each other.

"Brothers," said Little Lamb, "You both were afraid you would not have enough to eat. You both were selfish and forgot to look at your brother with love. You felt fear and anger and gave that to your brother, and that is what he gave back to you. Now let us try to see only the good and the love in each other...for surely that is what we will get in return."

Big Chipmunk looked down at Little Chipmunk and said, "If you were always hungry, and I always had enough to eat, why didn't you ask me for some extra nuts? Surely I would have given you some.

Little Chipmunk looked up at Big Chipmunk and said, I was afraid you would not give me any. You always seemed so angry with me."

"Yes, I was angry because I thought you were a thief. But now I can see you were just hungry and frightened, frightened you would not have enough to eat and frightened of me." Both Chipmunks looked at each other with new eyes.

"Truly," said Little Lamb "Anger only comes from fear. And if you but look and listen to your brother with love the fear and then the anger will disappear."

"From now on," said Big Chipmunk, "We will search for nuts together. You can help me find them and I can help you carry them."

"Then we can share them together," said Little Chipmunk. And off they ran together, happy to be friends and not enemies.

Little Lamb smiled for he could hear his Father's Voice in his heart saying, "Your brothers forgave each other for they saw the truth: Anger comes from fear and fear disappears when love is shared."

With that Little Lamb opened his eyes and the mist of the dream cleared. He was back in his Father's world of love, peace and happiness.

The Choice

Little Lamb entered the dream world again. His work was not finished as long as his brothers still forgot the real world of God.

Little Lamb and Beaver walked together through the forest. The sun shone brightly through the trees.

"The sun is very bright," said Beaver. He could feel the heat of the sun on the top of his head and thought: The sun is always too hot. When I am hot I feel tired. And when I am tired I feel grumpy. The sun is always too hot.

While Beaver thought his thoughts, Little Lamb was thinking also: How wonderfully warm and nice is the sun. Look how bright and beautiful it makes the forest. Thank you, Father, for letting me see the beauty of the sun.

Little Lamb and Beaver continued down the path in the forest. Soon they became hungry and began to look for something to eat. Beaver thought: Every time I am hungry I must look for food to eat. I must dig in the dirt for roots. I must always work. And when I work I feel tired. And when I am tired I feel grumpy.

Little Lamb also thought: Look at all this nice green grass to eat. Look at all the roots in the ground for my friend to eat. How wonderful is God Who gives us all we need. Thank you, Father.

After the friends had eaten, they grew tired and decided to rest. As Beaver lay on the ground he thought: Listen to all those insects buzzing. Listen to all those birds chirping. What an awful noise. How will I be able to rest if I must listen to this racket?

Little Lamb also lay down to rest and he thought: Listen to my brothers, the insects, buzzing. Listen to my brothers, the birds, chirping. How beautiful are the songs of life. Thank you, Father, for sending me such a wonderful lullaby.

Later in the day Little Lamb and Beaver met another beaver by a stream.

"Please help," asked the other beaver. "This log is too big for me to lift by myself and I must put it in the stream to help build my house."

As Little Lamb and Beaver helped their brother lift the log Beaver thought: Look at all this work I must do now. The log is getting my fur dirty and the water of the stream is making me wet and cold. And when I am dirty and wet and cold I get grumpy.

Little Lamb was also thinking as he helped his brother: How cool the water is as it washes the dirt off my wool. How nice it is to help my brother. Thank you, Father, for giving me this chance to help a friend, and for giving me the gift of my friend's thankful smile.

Later that evening Beaver heard Little Lamb saying, Thank you, Father, for a most beautiful and happy day."

"How can you say this day was beautiful and happy?" exclaimed Beaver. "The sun was too hot. It was hard to find food to eat. The noise of the birds and insects kept me awake, and I got dirty and wet and cold lifting that log."

"But don't you see that is how you decided to see the day," said Little Lamb. "Now listen to how I saw the day: The sun was warm and beautiful. The grass was sweet and plentiful. The birds and insects sang me a lullaby and our brother gave us the gift of his loving smile. And for all this I am very thankful."

Beaver's eyes began to light up. "You know Little Lamb, it wasn't what I did today, but how I decided to look at it. I chose to see only unhappiness in all that we did, and I was grumpy and unhappy. You chose to see only happiness in all that we did, and you were happy."

"Now you see," said Little Lamb smiling. "You decided whether to be happy or not. God our Father gives us only love and goodness. It is up to us to decided if we want to see that love and goodness.

And as Beaver looked around him he saw the shining stars and felt the warm night breeze as soft as a blanket on his fur and said, "Thank you Father, for this beautiful night."

And Beaver and Little lamb smiled.

Happiness

Little Lamb walked through the mist of the dream. His brothers were waiting for him. They had questions for him to answer.

Little Lamb sat in the center of the circle. All his brothers who lived in the forest sat around him and listened. "'Little Lamb," called one of the animals, "Tell us about happiness."

Little Lamb looked at all his friends and smiled, "First let me ask you what you think happiness is."

Gray Squirrel looked at Little Lamb and said, "Happiness is having piles and piles of seeds and nuts. When I have all the seeds and nuts in the world, then I will be happy."

"Are you happy now?" asked Little Lamb.

"No," said Gray Squirrel. "But I will be when I get all the seeds and nuts in the world."

Fat Robin with tears in her eyes said, "I just lost happiness. This past summer all my babies were with me as I helped them grow big and strong. Now they are gone to have their own families and with them went my happiness."

"Are you happy now?" asked Little Lamb.

"No," said Fat Robin. "When my children were with me I had happiness, but now they are gone and my happiness is gone also."

Pack Rat spoke up next. In his arms he held all the odd things he had found that day: a stone, an acorn and a small tin can. "I am happy when I have with me all the things that I find. It took me a long time to find these things. I won't let anybody take them from me. As long as I have them I am happy."

"Are you happy now?" asked Little Lamb.

"Now I am happy because I have all my things. But I am afraid that I will lose them." And so Pack Rat sat down clutching his things close to him, frightened that he would lose his happiness.

Little Lamb looked at his friends and said, "Gray Squirrel is not happy now because he has not found happiness yet. Fat Robin is not happy now because she has just lost happiness. Pack Rat thinks he is happy because he has all his things, but he is frightened that he will lose them. So if he is frightened, can he really be happy?"

And Pack Rat said, I guess I am not really happy because I am afraid I will lose those things that I thought were happiness. Tell us, Little Lamb, how we can be happy now."

Little Lamb smiled at his brothers and said, "Happiness is not something, or someone, or someplace. Happiness just is, inside you. When you feel God's love in your heart you feel happy. When you want to share God's love with all your brothers you feel happy. And when you feel happy inside your happiness shines on everyone you meet. When you feel happy inside no matter who you are with, where you are or what you have, you will be happy because you carry it around with you."

"Are you happy now, Gray Squirrel?" asked Little Lamb.

"Yes, I am happy. It's not the nuts and seeds will make me happy, only me," said the squirrel.

"Are you happy now, Fat Robin?" asked Little Lamb.

"Yes, I am happy, because I love my children whether they are with me or not," said Fat Robin.

"Are you happy now, Pack Rat?" asked Little Lamb.

"Yes, I am happy, because if I am happy inside myself it doesn't matter if I have my things or lose my things, I will still be happy."

***And as they all sat in the circle,
God's love was in them and around them
and they were all very happy.***

Love

Little Lamb walked through the mist of the dream and came upon a lovely pond. Two swans began to swim toward him.

"Hello, Little Lamb," said Mr. Swan. "I would like you to meet my new wife whom I love very much." Mrs. Swan smiled sweetly at Little Lamb.

"Hello, Mr. and Mrs. Swan," said Little Lamb. "You. both seem very happy together."

"Yes, we are happy," said the swan, "because we love each other.

Little Lamb smiled at his friends and asked, "Can you tell me why you love each other?"

Mr. Swan laughed and said, "That is easy, it is because my wife is so pretty."

And Mrs. Swan said, "It is because he is so handsome."

"Then tell me," asked Little Lamb, "if your wife were to lose her beauty and your husband were to become ugly, would you still love each other?"

The swans smiled at each other and said, "Yes, we would still love each other very much."

"Then tell me again," asked Little Lamb, "why you love each other?"

Mr. Swan thought for a moment and said, "I know that if I need help my wife will be there to help me and that is why I love her."

Little Lamb asked, "If your wife could not be there when you needed her, would you still love her?"

"Yes, I would love her even if she could not be there to help me."

And Mrs. Swan smiled at her husband.

"Then tell me again," asked Little Lamb, "why do you love each other?"

Mr. Swan thought again and said, "She will be a good mother for our children."

And Mrs. Swan said, "He will be a good father for our children."

Little Lamb looked at his friends and asked, "What if you do not have any children, will you still love each other?"

The two swans looked at each other and said together, "Yes, we would still love each other very much. But tell us Little Lamb, if we loved each other even though we were ugly, or could not help each other, or could not have children, then why would we love each other so much?"

"You do not love because of any reason. Love is a precious gift given by God to all His children. When we feel God's love in us and around us we can give that love to all our brothers and sisters. You have decided to feel and enjoy God's love together. Enjoy God's gift of love. Sharing is the nicest part of any present."

And as Little Lamb waved goodbye the two swans swam off happily.

In his heart Little Lamb could hear God's Voice, "As long as My children remember the love which I give to each of them, then they shall always have love to give and share with each other.

Judgment

Lion was waiting for Little Lamb as he walked through the mist into the dream.

"Little Lamb," cried Lion, "You must help me."

"How can I help you?" asked Little Lamb.

Lion looked sadly at Little Lamb and said, "All the animals come to me with their problems.

They want me to decide who is right and who is wrong. They want me to punish the wrongdoer, but I am not sure I am doing the right thing."

"Tell me about it," said Little Lamb.

And so Lion told him about two baby possums. "They are always arguing," said Lion. "Their mother asked me to decide what to do."

Little Lamb smiled at Lion and said, "We can never make decisions by ourselves. We can only ask our Father to help us find an answer. For in His goodness and mercy He will send the answer to every problem."

Little Lamb and Lion closed their eyes and listened for their Father's answer. In their hearts they heard these words.

"Listen carefully My children. justice is being fair. Only through love can everyone gain and no one lose. Leave all judgment to Me, for I love my children and loving completely and equally is the only judgment there can be."

And so Little Lamb and Lion went to where the animals were waiting for them. Mother Possum was crying quietly. The baby possums waited near her.

Lion sat down on his rock and began, "You are here to ask my judgment on your problem. Both of you baby possums continue to fight and argue. Your mother is unhappy and you are unhappy. Let us solve this problem by asking our Father what to do."

And so Little Lamb and Lion went to where the animals were waiting for them. Mother Possum was crying quietly. The baby possums waited near her.

Lion sat down on his rock and began, "You are here to ask my judgment on your problem. Both of you baby possums continue to fight and argue. Your mother is unhappy and you are unhappy. Let us solve this problem by asking our Father what to do."

And so they all closed their eyes and asked their Father for help. Each one of them heard an answer in his heart.

Lion looked up and said, "My answer is to leave all judgment to our Father for His judgment is to love everyone equally. All must gain and none must lose. Punishment makes losers. Love creates winners."

Mother Possum looked up and said, "my answer is to love both of my children equally and trust in their love for each other. For through their own love they will decide what to do."

As the baby possums smiled at one another the large possum said, "My answer is to stop and ask our Father what to do whenever we start fighting."

The smaller possum then said, "And when we listen to God's answer He always shows us His love and then we want to share that love with each other. Who could stay angry when he is sharing love?" The two possums smiled at each other again.

Lion looked kindly at the possums and said, "We have asked our Father for help. And his judgment is to love equally and to trust in the sharing of that love. Go now and play. We have all learned our lessons well today."

As the possum family ran off into the forest, Little Lamb and Lion sat together happily. In their hearts they could feel God's love and wisdom, the only true judgment.

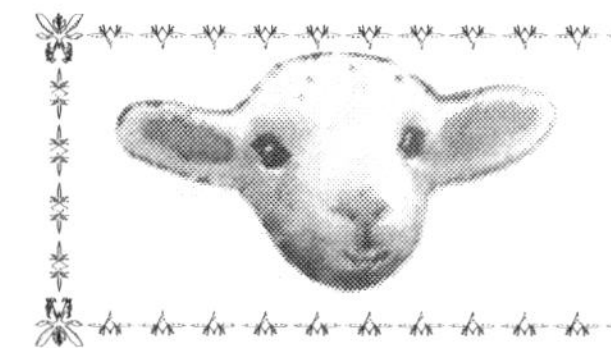

The Miracle

"Little Lamb ," called God. "Yes, Father," answered Little Lamb. "One of your brothers is dreaming and needs your help. In the dream he has forgotten his perfection which I gave him. Sleep, Little Lamb, and dream. Go into the dream and help your brother."

And in the dream Little Lamb opened his eyes. Long shadows covered the forest floor. Little Lamb could hear someone crying.

"Oh! Oh! My leg is broken. It hurts so much." Lying on the mossy ground was a spotted deer. Her eyes were closed with pain and her back leg was bent oddly.

Little Lamb walked over to the deer quickly. Scurrying around her was a little mouse. "Oh my, oh my," Mouse kept saying. "Miss Deer is much too big for a little mouse like me to move. Oh my, how can I help her?"

Owl sat on a branch overhead moaning, "No one can help her now. It is the end for her. If she can't run she will never be able to protect herself or find food to cat. No one can help her now."

And with that the deer cried more loudly for she was frightened and in pain.

Little Lamb looked down at the deer and smiled gently. "I know Who can help you Miss Deer. If you will but listen and believe, your leg will be healed."

The deer looked up with hope in her eyes. "I will listen Little Lamb. I want to believe."

"Gather 'round, Mouse and Owl," called Little Lamb. "Your sister needs all our help. Together with our Father we will heal her leg." Mouse and Owl slowly came forward and sat next to Miss Deer. They all sat very quietly as Little Lamb spoke.

“God our Father is love. He can only create loving things and He created you. God our Father is perfect. He can create only perfect things and He created you. Do you believe that our Father is perfect and loving and creates only perfect and loving things?” asked Little Lamb.

Mouse felt God’s kiss in the warmth of the sun and said, “Yes, I believe.”

Owl listened to God’s song in the sound of the buzzing insects and said, “Yes, I believe.”

Miss Deer looked at the other animals and saw them each glowing with God’s love and said, “Yes, I do believe.”

As they all sat feeling each other’s love and perfection the mist of the dream began to clear and they could see where they really were. Here was God’s perfect world. They had never left it. And for a holy instant Little Lamb, Miss Deer, Mouse and Owl were awake again in the peace and perfection of their Father’s world. But an instant doesn’t last and when they looked again they were back in the dream. But something wonderful had happened.

“Look! Look!”’ exclaimed Miss Deer. “My leg is healed. It doesn’t hurt any more. I can even walk on it.” And as the other animals watched, Miss Deer rose up on her legs and began to dance about merrily.

“It’s a miracle,” said Mouse.

“How is this possible?” asked Owl.

Little Lamb smiled. “Truly, through God’s love anything is possible. We saw ourselves loving and perfect as our Father made us. And so God gave us the gift of a miracle, so we may remember His love and our perfection.”

The breeze gently ruffled Little Lamb’s wool. As Little Lamb opened his eyes he saw that he was awake and in his Father’s world once more.

“You have done well today, My Son, “ said his Father’s Voice within his heart. “Today, for a holy instant, your brothers awoke from their dream and felt the love which I always have for them, and through that love was the gift of a miracle given.”

Through the Mist

"Little Lamb , Little Lamb. Help me. I am alone and frightened. Little Lamb, please help me." Little Lamb heard the call for help and drifted into the dream. He would come and he would help his brother in need.

Raccoon huddled close to the ground. His little body shook and shook with fear. All around him swirled a dark mist. All around him were dark angry looking clouds.

Little Lamb appeared at Raccoon's side. "I am so alone and afraid," Raccoon told Little Lamb.

"What are you afraid of?" asked Little Lamb.

"Don't you see? All around are dark clouds. All around the mist is so dark I cannot see through it. When I look closely at the mist I see things," said Raccoon shaking more and more as he looked around him.

"What things do you think you see in the mist?" asked Little Lamb.

"I see all the things I am afraid of. When I look in the mist I see my-self
getting hurt. I see myself alone with no one to love me. I am so afraid. What shall I do?" And Raccoon looked up at Little Lamb and his eyes filled with fear and unhappiness. Little Lamb's heart went out to his friend. He knew just what he must do to help Raccoon.

"Do you have faith in my love for you?" Little Lamb asked Raccoon.

"Yes I do," said Raccoon.

"Do you want to leave these misty nightmares behind you and walk into the light?" asked Little Lamb.

"Yes, I do," said Raccoon hopefully.

"Then walk with me but a little way. Walk with me through the mists of the dream for that is what you see. Your nightmares are not real. They are only reflections of your fears in the mist around you. Just as a mirror will reflect your frowning face, so also will the mists around you reflect your fearful thoughts. Follow me and see how unreal your fears are." And Little Lamb began to walk forward through the dark clouds.

Raccoon wanted to believe Little Lamb for he knew Little Lamb loved him. And so he gathered up his courage and followed Little Lamb into the dark clouds.

As they walked side by side the mist began to part. All the frightening nightmares Raccoon saw in the mist began to disappear.

"Look!" cried Raccoon. And through the mist Raccoon could see the shining light. The closer they came to the light, the less mist there was until soon they walked together into the bright, loving light. All the mist was gone and all the frightening nightmares with it.

Raccoon looked up into the shining light. God's warm love surrounded him. Fear was gone and only happiness and peace remained in his heart.

Raccoon looked at Little Lamb and said with surprise, "My nightmares weren't real were they? As soon as I saw the light and followed it the mist began to disappear. Now I can see where I really am. I am in God's world and I was here all the time. I just didn't see it."

Little Lamb smiled, "Yes Raccoon. Just as the warmth of the sun makes the morning mist disappear, so too will the warmth of God's love make your misty nightmares disappear."

As Little Lamb and Raccoon stood together surrounded by the light of God's love they could hear God's Voice in them and around them saying," Welcome. I have been waiting for you to awake. Come and be at peace in the real world of love and happiness."

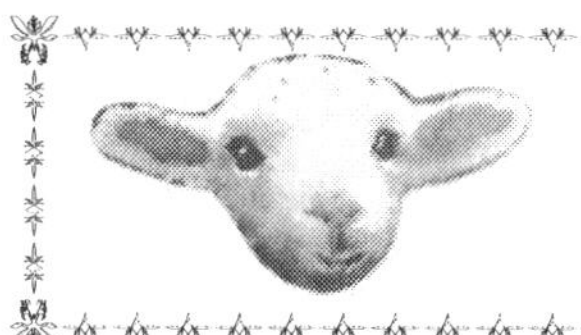

Life Forever

"Little Lamb, called God. "Your work is almost finished. Go into the dream world again. Your brothers need to know that life lasts forever."

As Little Lamb entered the dream he could hear Miss Deer talking loudly. "But it was a miracle. For a holy instant Little Lamb, the other animals and I were in God's real world and my broken leg was healed."

"I don't believe it," yelled Antelope, his antlers quivering with anger. "It was all a trick. Miracles can't really happen and this is the only world there is!" And with that Antelope turned to Little Lamb. "It is all your fault for giving these wild ideas to the animals."

In his anger Antelope lowered his antlers and butted Little Lamb, pushing him down to the ground. As Little Lamb fell his head hit a large stone and he lay very still.

For a moment there was frightened silence. Then Miss Deer began to cry. "Little Lamb is dead. Little Lamb is dead." And she began to cry more loudly.

All the other animals began to gather around, some of them crying, but all of them frightened.

Through the mist of the dream Little Lamb watched his friends standing and crying around his body. Little Lamb spoke to God his Father without words, "What shall I do now Father? All my brothers are sad and frightened because I have left my body. They think that I have died and am alive no more."

God spoke to Little Lamb," Go back into the dream Little Lamb. Show them that the body is just part of the dream. Show them that they use the body for learning. Show them that I have truly made them perfect and that there is no death, only beautiful life."

"My brothers," called Little Lamb to his friends in their hearts. "There is no death, for I am still alive."

Miss Deer looked around and said hopefully, "But where are you Little Lamb? I can hear your voice in my heart but I cannot see you. Your body is so quiet."

And as the other animals also heard Little Lamb within their hearts and listened, Little Lamb said, "I am here with you always, even as our Father is always with you. I am in the air you breathe, the water you drink, the clouds you look at and the grass you stand on. I am in your hearts, for this is where God's real world is. And here there is life forever."

As the animals watched, Little Lamb's body began to move slightly. His eyes began to flicker and his chest moved with deep breaths. Antelope exclaimed, "He lives! Little Lamb lives! He has come back to life."

Little Lamb stood up slowly and smiled at all his friends. As he looked around he could see Miss Deer smiling with happiness and love. Antelope's eyes were large with wonder and delight. And all the animals were quiet and filled with happy surprise.

"Truly," said Antelope. "Miracles do happen for I can see now that God's world is always around us."

"Yes," said Miss Deer. "And in God's world we are all perfect."

Little Lamb smiled at his friends and said, "Yes, our Father's world is filled with love and beauty. And in His world there could never be death, only beautiful life which lasts forever."

As the animals stood watching Little Lamb, a large beam of light fell on Little Lamb and he seemed to glow. And in their hearts all the animals could hear God's Voice saying, "This is your brother in whom I am well pleased. Today you are in My real world together. Come and enjoy the beauty and love I give to all of you.

For I love each and every one of My children and give you all the gift of life forever."

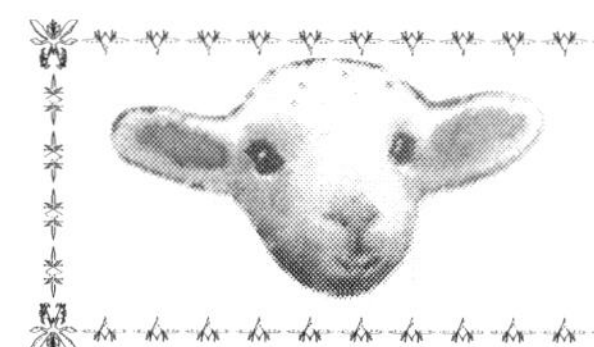

And Who Shall Save Us?

All the animals of the forest were waiting for Little Lamb. In the center of the circle was a large stone for Little Lamb to sit on. And on the stone was a crown made of white daisies. The animals were quiet as they waited for Little Lamb to appear. He entered the dream and saw his brothers waiting for him.

Fat Robin came forward and met Little Lamb. She said, "Come sit on the stone in the center of the circle. This will be your throne. And here is a crown of daisies to place on your head."

Little Lamb looked at his friends, "Why have you made a throne and crown for me?"

Fat Robin answered, "We want you to be our king. We want you to lead us and make our decisions for us. For you are wise and loving."

Then Miss Deer spoke up, "You have the power to perform miracles."

And Bear said, "You speak with God. You are His Son. Therefore we want to worship you."

Little Lamb looked around him sadly. "My brothers," he said, "I speak with God and when I listen to His Word I am wise and loving. But you cannot worship me. For though I am God's Son, so are you also."

"We are all the Sons of God and He has given His love and power and wisdom to all His children. I cannot make your decisions for you. You must listen for God's Voice yourself. I am powerful and wise because I listen to God's Voice, and He tells me what to do."

"But Little Lamb," called Miss Deer, "You perform miracles."

Gently Little Lamb said, “No, Miss Deer. I do not perform miracles. Miracles are a gift from God because we remembered His love for us and the perfection He gave us.”

Then Antelope spoke up, “You were dead and you came to life again. Surely that is something special only you can do?”

Little Lamb smiled at Antelope and said, “God does not die, for God lives forever. I am God’s Son, just as you are. I live forever and so do you.”

“Then who shall lead us back to God? Who shall take us to heaven? Who shall save us?” asked all the animals.

As they sat quietly waiting for the answer, God’s Voice spoke to each and everyone of them in his heart.

“My children, you are all saviors of the world. You are all My children and together, only together, shall My love be shared and completed. When you see My love in each of your brothers, then you shall know Me. When you give My love to each of your brothers then you shall know heaven. Who can save you? Why you can. For together with your brothers you shall save the world.”

Miss Deer looked at Fat Robin and Antelope and said, “You are my brothers, and we are all God’s children. Where His children are, so is He. Now I know where heaven is. It is right here, right now!”

And the animals looked at each other with love and understanding. God was with His children and they were in heaven with Him.

Together at Last

God spoke to Little Lamb in his heart, "All your brothers and sisters are ready to come home now. Go into the last dream and lead my children Home." As Little Lamb walked through the mist of the dream he could see all the animals of the forest waiting for him.

The sun shone gently on each brother and sister making them glow with their Father's love. They smiled at Little Lamb and each other. And Little Lamb could feel God's gift of love in them and around them. Little Lamb looked at all his brothers and sisters and said, "You have all learned your lessons here in the dream. The time for sleeping and dreaming is over. Let us all awake and go into our Father's world together."

Little Lamb turned to Gray Squirrel, Bear and Large Goose, "What lesson did you learn so that you may awake into the real world?"

And the three animals smiled and answered together, "We must only ask for the answers to our problems and then listen for our Father's loving Voice. For in our Father's love is the answer to all our questions."

Little Lamb smiled and said, "Come with me into our Father's world."

Next Little Lamb looked at the two chipmunks and asked, What lesson did you learn so that you may awake into the real world?"

The chipmunks said, "We forgave each other. Anger comes from fear and fear disappears when love is shared."

Little Lamb smiled and said, "Come with me into our Father's world."

The Beaver stood up next as a clear, bright beam of light fell on his head, and he said, "My lesson was to choose happiness. God gives me only love and goodness. It was up to me to decide if I wanted to see that love and goodness."

"Then come with me into our Father's world," said Little Lamb.

Miss Deer, followed by Mouse and Owl, stepped forward and said, "Together we left this dream for a holy instant and saw God's real world. Through the gift of God's love a miracle was given to me and my broken leg was healed. It is time for us to return to our Father's world forever."

Little Lamb smiled and said, "Then come with me."

As Little Lamb looked around at the other animals the two swans spoke up, "Our lesson is to share God's love together." And they smiled lovingly at each other.

Gray Squirrel, Fat Robin and Pack Rat all said together, "Happiness is inside you. When you feel God's gift of love you feel happy and want to share it with everyone."

Little Lamb smiled and said, "You have learned your lessons well. Come with me into our Father's real world."

Lion spoke up next, "Justice is being completely fair, and only love can make everyone win and no one lose." Lion and all the animals felt God's judgment in their hearts. They were all brothers and sisters and could feel their Father's love equally.

Antelope walked forward quietly and slowly looked around. "Yes, let us all go home to our Father, for in the dream we see nightmares filled with death. We see anger and fear in our brothers and we feel anger and fear in our hearts. But in God's real world there is only love, peace, forgiveness, perfection and beautiful life forever."

Through the mist into the dream appeared Raccoon. "Hello friends. I have come back into the dream once more to help Little Lamb bring you Home. Once before he helped me go through the mist and I learned my lesson: All the scary things I thought I saw in the dream were just reflections of my own fears."

Little Lamb smiled at all his friends and said, "The time has come. Let us walk but a little way together." And so they did. Through the mist they walked toward the bright light of their Father's love. As they walked the mist began to disappear and bright, loving light surrounded them. In their hearts they could all hear their Father's Voice. "Welcome home. The time for sleep and nightmares is over. Now is the time to awaken and see My real world. For I have created it with love as a most precious gift for My children. Come and enjoy what has always been yours."

And into their Father's world the animals came,
filled with happiness,
love and perfection.

The
Children's Workbook

"Bring the little children to Me,
for in their innocence love is born."

INTRODUCTION

These meditations are sent to each of you so you may bring the truth home again to the little souls with whom you are working. Whether you are parent or teacher, your role is one of love and forgiveness. As you meditate with your charge you will experience the awareness of God through each other. Each meditation should be practiced at the end of the lesson; or at home in the morning and evening. This should be a time of quiet, warmth and tenderness, a most profound moment together; and
together will you reach God.

Each lesson will be completed with a quiet period. This will allow students and teacher to meld together in the silence of God's love. This will be the time for the children's meditation. Children frequently develop talents and abilities in adapting to meditation, but most will not be able to sit quietly for long. Here is the secret to children's meditation: short, understandable and loving. The message will be loud and clear to each little soul listening with his heart. Be not disturbed if the children's reactions are not what you expect. Each child's body reacts differently to stimulation, including the spiritual kind. Bring patience, love and forgiveness with you to the meditation. Allow each child to express himself individually, without judgment.

Your group meditation should take place at the end of your lesson. Now is a quiet time for them to spend with you. They need not close their eyes, though it may help. The message of love will still make its way through the layers of ego to the heart of each little soul.

Read the meditation slowly and clearly. Then repeat the key phrases together. Ask the children to remember this idea all week, or until your next lesson. Now your tasks are finished for the day. Send your little ones home. Your lesson has been learned at the same time the little ones learned theirs.

1

"God is love.
God can only create loving things,
And God created you."

Think for a moment about who you are and from where you come. Look at your father and then look at yourself. Does your father have hands and feet? So do you. Does your father have arms and legs? So do you. Can your father smile and laugh? So can you. Are you like your father? Yes, you are.

Now think about God, the Father of everyone and everything. God our Father is filled with love. He is love. You cannot see love. You can only feel love. Are you like your Father? Yes, you are. Feel your Father's love. For you are truly your Father's Son, and as He is filled with love, so are you also.

(Now read aloud together)

"God is love.
God can only create loving things,
And God created me."

2

"God gives only kindness and love,
And God gives you everything."

How do you show love? You show love by doing loving things. How does God your Father, who loves you, show His love? He gives you kindness, happiness, peace and joy.

(Now read aloud together)

"God gives only kindness and love,
And God gives me everything."

#3

"Within my head God talks;
Within my heart God walks."

Where is God our Father? Don't look far, for He is inside you. He is that bright light of love which makes you what you are. He is the center of you.

Now listen quietly for His Voice to help you. He is always inside you and He shall speak to you if you would just listen with your heart. Isn't it nice to know you are never alone?

(Now read aloud together)

"Within my head God talks;
Within my heart God walks."

4

"Happy or sad,
Loving or scared;
Who decides? You do."

Look around you. Is the world bright and beautiful?
Or is it dark and ugly?
Do you see friends or do you see enemies?
Do you feel happy and peaceful,
or do you feel lonely and frightened?
The room you see is only a room.
You decide if it's ugly or beautiful.
The people you see each day are all your
brothers. You decide if they are your friends or enemies.

If you feel lonely and frightened then that is what you have decided to be.
Now let's decide to be happy and peaceful.
You are God's child.
You can be anything you want to be.

(Now read aloud together)

"Happy or sad,
Loving or scared;
Who decides? I do."

5

"Happy or sad, loving or scared;
Who helps you decide to be glad?
God does."

If we decide to be happy and decide to be frightened, then why would anyone stay frightened and unhappy? We could just decide to be happy. But we can't do it alone. We are part of God our Father Who is in us, and we must ask Him to help us decide to be happy.
Together with God we can do anything; we can be anything.
When we are together with God we are always happy.
The only decision we should make is to remember God is with us always and then we will always be happy.

(Now read aloud together)

"Happy or sad, loving or scared;
Who helps me decide to be glad?
God does."

6

"What makes a shadow scary or friendly?
Your mind does."

Your mind tells you what to think. Your mind tells you whether you like what you see or whether you don't like what you see.
Your eyes see shadows all around you.
Your mind decides if they are scary or friendly,
for you cannot touch a shadow and a shadow cannot touch you.
Shadows aren't real.
It is only what you decide to think about them
that makes them seem real.
When something or someone frightens you,
remember you are only seeing shadows.
Look for the light of God's love
and it will shine away all the scary
shadows that are not real.

(Now read aloud together)

"What makes a shadow scary or friendly?
My mind does."

7

"What makes your best friend a friend when you play,
but an enemy when you fight?
Your mind does."

He is loving and understanding;
therefore we are loving and understanding.
Your brother and you are the same.
But you can decide to see him differently.
You can decide not to like him. You can decide to fight with him.
Or you can decide to love him,
decide to understand him and decide to be happy together.
Why would you want to fight and be unhappy?
Your brother is just like you. He is loving and understanding,
and so are you.

(Now read aloud together)

"What makes my best friend a friend when we play
but an enemy when we fight?
My mind does."

LESSON 8

"Be a perfect mirror. Reflect God's love."

Shine brightly. Polish away all the thoughts of hate and anger.
Polish the mirror of your heart.
For just like a mirror you will reflect what is in your heart.
Polish away the dirt and grime and brightly reflect God's love.
His love is like a light shining brightly.
Let it shine on your heart and reflect love,
growing brighter with each loving thought and deed.

(Now read aloud together)

"I am a perfect mirror. Let me reflect God's love."

9

"Peace and love bring happiness
And joy your whole life through.
Peace and love bring happiness
Because God lives in you."

Whenever you are lost and afraid,
whenever things are not going your way,
remember this little prayer.
God your Father is always there, and where He is,
there you will find peace, joy and happiness.

(Now read aloud together)

"Peace and love bring happiness
And joy your whole life through.
Peace and love bring happiness
Because God lives in you."

10

"Where is God?
Where is He not?
You need not look far
For God is here, there and everywhere."

Listen quietly and you will hear your Father speak to you.
Look carefully with loving eyes
and you shall see where your Father lives.
He is not far away,
for He would never leave His children alone.
He is where you can always find Him.
He is right here, right now!

(Now read aloud together)

"Where is God?
Where is He not?
You need not look far
For God is here, there and everywhere."

11

"When God speaks the world listens;
His call of love breathes life to all."

Listen for your Father's Voice.
It will speak to you through the sparrow's
song; through the warm summer breeze;
through the happy laughter of children.
His Voice speaks to you of love and life.
For without love there is no life.
Listen for your Father's Voice;
It is within your heart, and there is love.

(Now read aloud together)

"When God speaks the world listens;
His call of love breathes life to all."

12

"Within our hearts God patiently waits;
Within God's heart we live and love."

God knows His children.
God understands His Sons.
God is always within you waiting patiently
for you to listen to His loving Voice.
Would a loving father leave his child alone and frightened?
Feel God within you and know that He is in you and you are in Him.

(Now read aloud together)

"Within our hearts God patiently waits;
Within God's heart we live and love."

13

"The wind—His gentle caress
The sun—His tender kiss
The rain—His tears of joy, cleansing and refreshing
The birds, insects and animals—Singing His songs of life
And all of this—His gift to His beloved children."

Thank you Father for Your love which you give to me, Your child.

(Now read aloud together)

"The wind—His gentle caress
The sun—His tender kiss
The rain—His tears of joy, cleansing and refreshing
The birds, insects and animals—Singing His songs of life
And all of this—His gift to His beloved children."

14

"Speak only of love
And only God's Voice will be heard."

Tell the world about God's love
and you become a tool for God's work.
Hear His Voice telling you what to do
and then let His words be yours when you speak.
He knows what is good and right.
He knows what is loving.
Listen to Him and speak only what you hear in your heart.
Look how easy it is.
And see how happy it makes you.

(Now read aloud together)

"I will speak only of love
And only God's Voice will be heard."

15

"Feel only God's peace
And heaven will surround you."

God is always here to guide and protect you.
He will keep you safe and happy.
All you need do is listen for His loving Voice
and feel His loving touch within you and around you.
Where is heaven, but in your hearts.
You need not look far.
For where God is, so also is heaven.

(Now read aloud together)

"I feel only God's peace
And heaven surrounds me."

16

"I am one.
You are, too.
Behold the three: God the Father, you and me.
Together we make love's trinity."

Behold the Three: God the Father you and me.
This is what love is all about.
You are part of God; you are His child.
Your brother is part of God;
he is God's child also.
If you are to love God, you must love all that is a part of God.
And so we must love our brothers.
God loves everything that is His.
And we are His Children Whom He loves.
Behold the Three;
God the Father you and me.
Together we make love's trinity.
Together we are one.

(Now read aloud together)

"I am one.
You are, too.
Behold the three: God the Father, you and me.
Together we make love's trinity."

17

"Make each day your very best;
Make each minute one of peace and rest;
Make each second a moment with God;
It's the path to joy; it's a happy heart."

You have two choices today.
You can remember God is with you now,
or you can forget He is here.
If you choose to forget He is with you,
you will feel lost, alone and frightened.
But if you remember He is never away from you,
always loving and always guiding and protecting,
then you shall be happy and safe.

(Now read aloud together)

"Make each day your very best;
Make each minute one of peace and rest;
Make each second a moment with God;
It's the path to joy; it's a happy heart."

18

"Each one of us is like each other...
Part of a whole; each part a brother."

Where do you end and your brothers begin?
Where does God end and where does He begin?
You may look different.
You may look like you are separated from your brothers,
but you are not just your body.
You are much, much more.
You are spirit. You cannot see or touch spirit.
You can only feel spirit with your heart.
This is where God is. This is what God is.
He is spirit and so are you.
Together with God and your brothers you are one.
You are parts of the Whole and together you complete God's love.

(Now read aloud together)

"Each one of us is like each other...
Part of a whole; each part a brother."

19

"Whenever you feel all alone
Just look and see Who's with you;
With every breath that you breathe in
Feel God's touch, He's in you."

He is your helper. He is your friend.
He is the one who helps you all the time
whenever you ask.
He loves you and He is always with you.
Breathe deeply and feel His love filling you.
You are His Son whom He loves.

(Now read aloud together)

"Whenever I feel all alone
I just look and see Who's with me;
With every breath that I breathe in
I feel God's touch, He's in me."

20

"A smile, a look, a helpful word...
Prayers of love from brother to brother."

What's the nicest way of saying I love you?
It may be just a smiling face to give to someone sad.
It may be just a look of love
when someone feels they're bad.
It may be just a word or two to help someone who's feeling blue.
It doesn't matter what it is
as long as love is sent from you.

(Now read aloud together)

"A smile, a look, a helpful word...
Prayers of love I give to my brothers."

21

"Whenever someone seems to say,

'I don't love you, go away.'
Look deep within, for love is there,
Hiding far below his fear.
Fear that you don't love him too,
But you do love Him, and he loves you.
So whenever someone seems to say:

'I don't love you, go away,'
Look deep within for love is here,
Shining bright, forever near."

Don't be fooled by someone's angry face and words.
Listen very carefully.
For what they are really saying is that they are afraid
and feel unloved.
Their anger is a call for help and love.
Let us help all our brothers.
All we need to do is love them.
Who could stay angry when love surrounds him?

(Now read aloud together)

"Whenever someone seems to say,

'I don't love you, go away.'
Look deep within, for love is there,
Hiding far below his fear.
Fear that you don't love him too,
But you do love Him, and he loves you.
So whenever someone seems to say:

'I don't love you, go away,'
Look deep within for love is here,
Shining bright, forever near."

22

"To know your heart,
Look into your brother's eyes."

Your brother is a mirror of yourself. What do you see there?
Do you see anger, fear, sadness?
Or do you see happiness, peace, joy?
If you do not like what you see in your brother,
then look within yourself and change it there.
Your brother is just a mirror of yourself.
Feel happy and loving, and you will see happiness and love
reflected in your brother also.

(Now read aloud together)

"To know my heart,
I must look into my brother's eyes."

23

"Hold the thought of hurt and pain
And there you're trapped and there remain.
But hold the thought of joy and health
And know God's peace, His love, His wealth."

You are a Son of God. You can be whatever you want to be.
Choose happiness and you will be happy.
Choose fear and anger and you will be unhappy.
Choose sickness and pain and you will have those also.
And all you need to do is think about it, and it will be yours.
Which do you want?
Happiness or unhappiness; love or fear; health or sickness?
God wants you to be happy, loving and healthy.
Let's think His thoughts.

(Now read aloud together)

"If I hold the thought of hurt and pain
I will be trapped and there will remain.
But now I hold the thought of joy and health
And I know God's peace, His love, His wealth."

24

"All our minds are one—We touch.
We touch in thought,
We touch in love.
For love is thought expressed to all."

We are all God's Sons. We are all connected by love.
And what is love but a thought.
We think with our minds. And our minds are one.
All we need do is think of love
and we will be one with all our brothers
and with God all at once.
Isn't love wonderful?

(Now read aloud together)

"All our minds are one—We touch.
We touch in thought,
We touch in love.
For love is thought expressed to all."

25

"Open up your eyes and heart
Like petals on a flower.
Open up your eyes and heart
To feel God's love and power."

Have you really looked around you lately?
Have you really listened carefully?
What do you see and hear?
If you really look and listen you will hear God's Voice
calling to you in the rustle of the leaves,
or the roar of the freight train,
or the happy laughter of your friends and family.
He is always there.
Just look closely and listen.
You can hear Him now. He is saying "I love you."

(Now read aloud together)
"I open up my eyes and heart
Like petals on a flower.
I open up my eyes and heart
And feel God's love and power."

26

"You're in God's Mind
So think His thoughts."

If God is love, then what kind of thoughts would God have?
Why loving thoughts, of course.
If you are God's Son, then you are love also.
What kind of thoughts would you have?
Why loving thoughts, of course.
Listen to your Father's Voice and think His Thoughts with Him,
for they are your thoughts also.
They belong to you. Think love, for you are love.

(Now read aloud together)

"I'm in God's Mind
So I think His thoughts."

27

"Where is God's world?
Right here, Right now.
Can you see God's world?
Yes, with loving eyes, that's how."

Heaven isn't far away. Heaven is right here.
Every time you are filled with love and happiness
you are remembering your real home.
Every time you share love with your brothers
you are giving a piece of heaven to someone else
and heaven grows with the giving.
Where is heaven? Right here. Right now.

(Now read aloud together)

"Where is God's world?
Right here. Right now.
Can I see God's world?
Yes, with loving eyes, that's how."

28

"Be ever alert to God's own thoughts:
They are Thoughts of love.
They are Thoughts that heal.
They are Thoughts of oneness to know and to feel."

Listen carefully to the thoughts you think.
You will always know
when you
are thinking God's Thoughts with Him.
His Thoughts make you happy.
His Thoughts make you well.
His Thoughts are filled with love and joy.
His Thoughts are yours. All you need do is think them.

(Now read aloud together)

"Be ever alert to God's own thoughts:
They are Thoughts of love.
They are Thoughts that heal.
They are Thoughts of oneness to know and to feel."

29

"Pain and death
Or joy and life
The choice is yours."

Who decides what your body will be like?
Is it strong? Is it healthy? Is it weak? Is it sick?
What would God make your body like?
Would He make you sick? Never.
Would He make you weak? Never.
Would He make you strong and healthy? Of course!
He loves you. He gives you everything.
But it is up to you if you want to accept His gifts.
Which do you choose?

(Now read aloud together)

"Pain and death
Or joy and life.
The choice is mine."

30

"God's gift to you is life."

Life is more than breathing in and out.
Life is being happy.
Life is feeling
peace and joy.
Life is knowing God is always with you.
Life never ends. Life is for always.
And it is always yours.

(Now read aloud together)

"God's gift to me is life."

31

"Place your hands in God's And He will lead you home."

Your Father's loving hands are always there to help you.
In your heart you will hear His Voice,
guiding you and showing you the way.
And as you listen
you will feel His hands taking yours and leading you to safety.
God's home is your home.
God's home is heaven and you have never left it.

(Now read aloud together)

"I place my hands in God's
And He will lead me home."

32

"Heal yourself by asking God's help."

If God doesn't make you sick, then who does? You do.
You choose sickness or pain or unhappiness.
How can you become healthy and happy?
By simply changing your mind.
Can you do it alone. No, you can't.
That is why God is always there to help you.
All you have to do is ask.

(Now read aloud together)

"I heal myself by asking God's help."

33

"Change your mind—And change the world. Heal yourself—And the world is healed with you."

You are a part of God and God is a part of everything and everyone.
You are in God and God is in everything and everyone.
You are a Thought of God and God's Thoughts are everything and everyone.
You are never alone and what you think
and what you do affects everything
for you are a part of God.

(Now read aloud together)

"I change my mind—And I change the world.
I heal myself—And the world is healed with me."

34

"Your brother shares his thoughts with you.
Your thoughts are his; false or true.
True thoughts bring love,
False bring sorrow.
Which would you think?
Which would you follow?
Which would you give your brother as gifts?
Which would you want from
Your brother as presents?
Your brother shares his thoughts with you.
Your thoughts are his; false or trite
True thoughts bring love,
False bring sorrow."

Now let's say together:
"I give the gift of love to my brother."

35

"Sharing, helping, loving, feeling;
Thoughts of God; thoughts of healing."

God's Thoughts are always in your mind.
But sometimes we forget them.
All we must do is think of loving things we want to do for our brothers.
All we need think about is happiness, joy, sharing and helping.
These are God's Thoughts, and they are our thoughts too.
Help yourself and help your brother today.
How wonderful and how simple it is.

(Now read aloud together)

"By sharing, helping, loving, feeling,
I think God's Thoughts: I think of healing."

36

"Take the time to love your brother."

Look at all the things your mind thinks about all day.
Think about all the thoughts you have.
How many of your thoughts are about your brothers?
How many of your thoughts about your brothers are loving thoughts?
Let's spend more time thinking loving thoughts about our brothers.

(Now read aloud together)

"I will take the time to love my brother."

37

"Where will you find your Father? He is looking out from behind your brother's eyes."

God our Father is not far away.
God lives in you and He lives in me, and He lives inside your brother.
All you need do to find your Father and your Father's love is
to look closely at your brother.
There is love and there is happiness.
Look deep within your brother's eyes
and know His home and yours and mine.

(Now read aloud together)

"Where will I find my Father?
He is looking out from behind my brother's eyes."

38

"To find your Father
Look deep within your brother."

Do not ignore your brother's gift of love.
It is your Father's gift of love given through your brother.
There, in your brother is the home you have been looking for.
There, in your brother's love will you find the love you are looking for.
There is God; there is heaven; there is joy.

(Now read aloud together)

"To find my Father
I must look deep within my brother."

39

"Happiness is shared by all."

See how catchy a smile is.
See how catchy a laugh is.
Giggle and smile and the world wants to join you.
Now think about your smiling thoughts. They are catchy too.
Send the world some giggles and a smile.
You will feel good and the world will feel good with you.

(Now read aloud together)

"My happiness is shared by all."

40

"Open your eyes and see your brother...
Shining bright, shining clear;
A mirror of your love,
A reflection of your Father."

Your brother is the mirror for your love.
Let your love shine brightly
so it may reflect off your brother
and bless you with happiness.
See your brother as loved and loving
and you will be loved and loving also.

(Now read aloud together)

"I open my eyes and see my brother...
Shining bright, shining clear;
A mirror of my love,
A reflection of my Father."

41

"Who speaks to you when you're alone?
Who guides you and directs you home?
God does."

Now you know who loves you best.
Now you know where to find His love.
Now you know how to hear your Father's loving Voice.
Listen silently to His Voice, for it will show you the way home.
It will show you happiness and joy.
It is the Voice of Love."

(Now read aloud together)

"Who speaks to me when I'm alone?
Who guides me and directs me home?
God does."

42

"Remember who and what you are;
Remember you are God's own Son."

God is spirit. And so are you.
God is love. And so are you.
God gives happiness and joy; and this you receive.
God creates heaven; and that is your Home.
God is your Father, and you are His Son.
What a wonderful family we have!

(Now read aloud together)

"I remember who and what I am;
I remember I am God's own Son, and I am happy."

43

"Love bursts forth across your mind;
God's own love: It's yours...It's mine."

Feel the mighty power of love.
It brings you all you ever need.
It brings you love and happiness and peace.
It connects you with all your brothers.
It connects you with your Father.
Love is like the mighty rope that ties us all together.
Feel God's love and know it's yours forever.

(Now read aloud together)

"Love bursts forth across my mind;
God's own love: It's yours...It's mine."

44

"Open up your heart and know;
God is here and heaven is now."

We look all over to find the things that will make us happy.
Sometimes we think it will be a toy,
but soon we tire of it.
Sometimes we think it is a place to visit,
but the fun we have only lasts a moment.
You do not have to look far to find happiness.
Happiness is God, and God is always with you.
Happiness is heaven, and the home of heaven is in God's love.
Don't look far, for God is here and heaven is now.

(Now read aloud together)

"I open up my heart and know;
God is here and heaven is now."

LESSON 45

"Faith and trust, hope and love;
Prayers and gifts to God above."

God gives us everything.
He gives us the most precious gift of all—His love.
And His love will make us happy and peaceful.
What does God ask in return?
The only gift our Father wants is for us to have faith and trust in His love for us.
How simple it is.
All we need do is send love out from us
and we will receive God's gift of love in return.

(Now read aloud together)

"Faith and trust, hope and love;
Prayers and gifts to God above."

46

"Place your faith in God your Father.
He leads you home, you and your brother."

You cannot come home alone.
Your brother must come with you.
How can you and your brother go home together?
That is easy. Just send your brother love.
See him happy. See him healthy. See him perfect.
See him as a Son of God, just like you.
And then together will God your Father lead you home to heaven.

(Now read aloud together)

"I place my faith in God my Father.
He leads me home, me and my brother."

47

"Who guides us and directs us home?
Who knows our needs and joys?
Who gives us everything and more? God does."

Let God lead you home. Let God make you happy.
Let God give you everything you need.
The only thing you must do is open your heart to His loving Word.
And the Word is love.
Listen for his message.
In everything you think and do, listen for the love that is there.
Send that love from you to your brothers
and receive from God the blessings of heaven, now.

(Now read aloud together)

"Who guides me and directs me home?
Who knows my needs and joys?
Who gives me everything and more? God does."

LESSON 48

"We are God's Son.
We are love.
We are home, in heaven, now."

Are we our bodies? No, we are spirit.
Are all our thoughts God's thoughts?
No, only happy, loving thoughts are God's Thoughts.
Who decides whether we will think happy or unhappy thoughts? We do.
What are you really like? You are love, and love always brings joy.
Where is your home? Your home is in heaven, and heaven is right here, right now.
All you need do is feel loving and happy and you will find heaven, now.

(Now read aloud together)

"We are God's Son.
We are love.
We are home, in heaven, now."

49

"I am as God created me."
Did you really listen to what I just said?
"I am as God created me."
Say this with me now:

"I am as God created me."

Think about what that means. God created only love.
God gives only happiness and joy. God is your Father,
and you are like your Father.
Say this with me again:

"I am as God created me."
"I am perfect."
"I am love."
"I am God's Son."

Now let us say again one more time:
"I am as God created me."

50

"We go together to our Father's home."

Our lessons for the year are almost over.
We have learned Who our Father really is. We have learned who we really are.
We have learned it is our decision, not God's, to be happy or not.
We know God only gives love.
And we have learned the most important thing:
"We cannot reach our Father's home unless we take our brothers with us.
Show each of your brothers total love.
Give him your happiness and joy,
and together God will lead you home."

(Now read aloud together)

"We go together to our Father's home."

LESSON 51

"I am home."

Heaven is the home of happiness.
Heaven is filled with peace and love.
Heaven is deep within your heart. There is God our Father.
There, if we will but listen, is the message, that will give us everything we could ever want.
We have learned to listen and hear God's word of love.
We have learned to send His love out to all our brothers.
We have learned how to be in heaven right now.
We simply must choose to be happy and loving.
Where are you right now?

(Now read aloud together)

"I am home."

#52

"Come little children and you shall hear about your Father in heaven:"

"Where is heaven?"
(Now let the children answer)
But in my heart.

"How can you find heaven?"
(Now let the children answer)
But I must look within.

"How shall you know heaven?"
(Now let the children answer)
But God my Father will speak to me.

"How shall you hear your Father?"
(Now let the children answer)
But by keeping all my thoughts still.

"And what message shall your Father send you?"
(Now let the children answer)
But that I am a part of Him and He is everything.

"When will you know your Father?"
(Now let the children answer)
But I never knew Him not!

Epilogue...

You and your student have followed a steep path on a long journey.
Together you have stepped out of time by using time,
and you have come closer to the awareness of your true reality.

Remember only the joy this past year has brought you.
Look back only to see how far you have come
and realize the journey you made was helped by
One Who knows your needs and guided you along the path which you chose.

Now your work has just begun,
for now you have begun to feel alive.
Now you have begun to see your true role.
Now you have begun to assume your true function.
You are the savior of the world
and together with your student you will be saved.

Begin your work now.
For God is with you always
and it is His will with yours which will guide you home.

Instructions for Working with Children

INTRODUCTION

To all who would be teachers of young minds...

The tasks you are to perform will come down through the levels of awareness until the minds touch. Here you will seek salvation. Here you will seek oneness with those you help. Do not forget the reason for your function. The goal is understanding; the means will be love; the reward will be freedom.

Each child represents an aspect of yourself expressed uniquely. Each child answers the need to fulfill your function of forgiveness. Each child and teacher together fulfill the promise given by God to his Sons when the separation occurred. Now together you will complete the promise of oneness, the return to God.

The child's mind must be approached on two levels. First it must be gently opened to the thought patterns for which we are striving. This should be accomplished with extreme care and love, each petal gently unfolded as if by the loving kiss of the sun.

Each child, already formed spiritually, must be experienced uniquely. Through these experiences, you as teacher, will reverse roles and learn through the child's unquestioning faith in love. Some children already will have had the stamp of ego impressed firmly on their thought patterns, but even these will have the magnificent pliability to grow, expand and learn. On this second level you, the teacher, will learn.

Lessons can be planned through the material available to you. Each lesson will revolve around an important concept; but in all cases your own love and creativity, channeled through you from the Holy Spirit, should be the guiding factor.

Materials will become available to help you demonstrate concepts. But always remember that it will be the child himself who will supply the main ingredient in each lesson. Your job will be to listen, and by listening to the Holy Spirit within each child you will be witness to his growth.

Go forth and lead My children home. In their innocence love is born and through the loving expression of their lives My Word is sent forth. Fulfill your function with love and gratitude.

Your first lessons with any child will be to open his mind to the idea that heaven is within himself. He must begin to realize that the world around him will seem to change simply by his own change in attitude and perspective. The hell he thinks he lives, the nightmares experienced when awake or asleep, is his growing acceptance of ego and separation. He is learning to accept himself as a limited being, limited by his physical manifestation. Now will be the time for us to end his downward spiral into ego-orientation and reverse the cycle upward to the expansion of universal love.

The practical application of this will be to show him the way to look at things differently. For example: What makes a shadow friendly or scary?

His mind does. As each child looks through his own experiences your job will be to help him see the holiness within them. Use stories, personal experiences and supplemental material to illustrate your points. Allow the brightness of your spirit to shine through the clouds around each child and to help him bask in the love of his Father.

The following lessons will cover the child's budding awareness of his illusory world. This is important. Allow him free expression during these periods. When enough time is spent on acknowledging illusions, then the next stage of learning will take place.

Now his lessons on forgiveness will come. Through these lessons the child will learn the process of overlooking sin. For what he believes to be sin is simply illusion which in reality never occurred. The bedrock of this course is to teach forgiveness. Now comes the challenge of awakening the child's awareness of his brother's needs, and through his acceptance of his forgiven brother he will forgive himself. These lessons will cover much time and should be handled delicately. Within these lessons gentle counseling will take place. Provide ample opportunity for the children to counsel each other. Here they will begin their own work with their brothers. Your job as teacher will be to mediate and to guide the children's counseling among themselves rather than to lecture. Within these lessons you will form the fundamental approach to miracles. This will be the heart of your work.

Children are constantly functioning on a receptive level. This will allow you to dip deeply into the wellspring of wisdom which is harbored in each child's heart. Material specifically prepared for the young mind will be presented to each of you. The concrete not the abstract must be the learning format.

Through the Rays of Light will knowledge be opened.

ADAPTATION

Learning—Teaching

Working with children is one way of expressing and living the Word. We are one and through our acknowledgment of oneness we will begin to learn Truth. It will be through the path which each one seeks that his knowledge will become manifest. The children will learn and teach. Their paths have directed them to you their teacher. But where is that dividing line between teacher and student? Their learning sequence is correlated closely with yours. Learn well the lessons your students teach you for it is through their inner wisdom expressed to you that your growth will be assured.

Learning involves a reawakening to truths already held deeply within the heart. Awakening to these truths is our sole purpose here on earth. When each and everyone can be aware of his ultimate destiny, heaven will be proclaimed on earth and illusions will disappear from awareness.

Teaching involves the demonstration of what you are learning. It is through this reinforcement of your own lessons that you become witness of God's world for others. Do not confuse the two, learning and teaching, as opposites. For it is only through the combination of both that reality can be shared. Do not deny your existence by denying the truth hidden within each of your students. Their reality is yours. Their love is a reflection of your own. Teach well, for it is through your efforts that you will learn.

Take the child's hand and lead him through the brambles of illusions to the inner path of truth. Together reality will unfold, for it is only through your brother that you may reach salvation. Now go in peace and learn your lessons through teaching.

Learn well the concept you think you are teaching the child, for it is this very same lesson which you must learn also. Do not assume that because you are the "teacher" you have learned the lessons. You would not be teaching them if this were so.

Watch each student who comes before you closely. He is an expression of yourself which you have not allowed yourself to recognize. This is his purpose for being there, just as your presence is an opportunity for him to see aspects of himself reflected in you. Through the eyes of love you will experience Christ. See Christ in each of your students and thereby find Christ in yourself.

Oneness of God

Let us consider the problem of bringing these concepts to the young mind. At an inner level all children, as well as adults, are fully aware of Truth. It is only in its upward travel from the subconscious to conscious that much is lost and distorted. Here, in the ego-oriented realm, we analyze and choose those facts which will reinforce what our five senses record.

The idea of oneness with our brothers is an abstraction difficult for an adult to understand, but not impossible for a child. Spiritual awareness must be triggered. This is your role. Body or ego-orientation must be minimized and spiritual oneness emphasized.

In the child's mind God becomes an all powerful parental figure separated from him. Because of our limitation to the five senses His power seems to transcend ourselves. This can be either comforting or frightening. Help free the child from his fears and place all emphasis on God's love which surrounds him, fills him and guides him. Remember always to express God's love as something within rather than without. Bring the awareness of God's presence into correct focus. He is within. Your Self is within and so you are with God, in God and of God. Bring the awareness of his holiness upward to consciousness within the child and free him from the imprisoning ideas of ego.

The Holy Spirit's Guidance

Let the Holy Spirit guide you in all your work and you will then be able to teach your students to do the same. By allowing the Holy Spirit to guide you, you will be witness to the presence of God within rather than without.

Children need to know that there is something upon which they can depend. Their world, a magnified version of the adult world, is one of powerful adversaries. To this we must address our efforts. To the child, the whole world can be either a frightening enemy or adventurous friend. In either case his feelings of inadequacy are apparent. He seems to have little effect over his surroundings. The surroundings seem to affect him.

Reliance on the Holy Spirit's loving guidance must come next. Each child must be taught to look within himself and to listen for his Father's Voice within his heart. Here will be the answer to his problems and guidance for his decisions. The method will be teaching prayer and meditation. Individual and group meditation techniques must be taught. How peaceful the world would be if each adult and child spent just a few minutes with his Father unifying their spirits consciously.

Through individual prayer and with God's help the child will learn to find his own answers. Group meditation during your teaching periods will help solidify the unity of spirit so necessary to the concept of brotherhood. This is the heart of counseling: To pray together and hear God's Word simultaneously, the miracle occurring.

The Holy Spirit's function is the link between the inner self, or God awareness, with the outer self. Too often we forget to contact our innermost Self, the seat of heaven, the throne of God.

In teaching young minds to go within, it is necessary to help them discern the difference between ego-imaginings and true silence, the silent knowledge of truth. Teach them to release their awareness from daydreams of reality and come deep into full awareness of the real world. Peace, happiness, joy: These will be the guideposts for their journey within. Take the child gently to the door and help him knock. The Holy Spirit will help him open the door and walk within. Your job is to show him how to get there and how to ask. This will be accomplished through the simple prayers given at the end of each lesson. Discuss them; use them; allow the children a short quiet time to meditate on them. This will be the road to awareness. Thus time will be used to reach the Father.

Illusion

The child's mind is filled with fantasies. He lives in the active world of illusion building. You call them games. As adults you have forgotten you are still illusion building and still playing games. Games are of the ego. Spirituality of purpose is reality.

It is within the illusion that the child begins to see himself represented. The illusion becomes all his points of reference. He becomes a pawn of the illusion instead of its maker.

Your job as teacher will be to help the child out of this limited sphere and to help him to acknowledge his limitlessness. The first area to be approached will be thought. It will be through his awareness of the power of thought that he will gain conscious control over his environment. "The Choice"* will be an excellent starting place to begin discussion of what the mind can do. Here we have two points of view about one specific point of action. This idea can be expanded to include all of the child's experiences of the week or day. His friends can help him see the different ways of looking at his world. In this way all the children can widen their awareness of the power of thought and attitude. Now he begins to see how he forms his own happiness and unhappiness. His world brightens with the light of understanding. His consciousness begins to take direction from his Self through the Holy Spirit's guidance. He is now beginning to listen.

*(See the story "The Choice" in Little Lamb, Part I)

Thought

Now will be the time to introduce the all-encompassing aspects of thought: There are no private thoughts; there are no neutral thoughts. Each of these concepts must be approached separately and then brought together into the focus of forgiveness and the resultant miracle.

As the connected essence of Oneness we could no more think private thoughts than we could separate ourselves from our Father. We are spirit combined and indivisible, whole and holy, the Creation.

As we are part of God, so do we also have the power of God. He gives us the freedom, the glory and the power. We are the Thoughts of God and in His image are our thoughts powerful.

Choose your thoughts wisely: ego or spirit; fear or love; unhappiness or happiness. To which thought system do you wish to listen. These ideas and options must be presented to each child. He must become aware of the power of his thoughts and the necessity of listening to and choosing from the thought system which will bring him only happiness. Help him choose wisely for through your loving guidance will salvation be yours and his.

Now that he has become aware of his power he must also become aware of his responsibility.

Forgiveness

He must learn that only through forgiveness of his brother will he and his brother be saved. Show him that as he sees his brother's perfection he shall see his own. Help him to reflect God's love onto his brother so he may receive it in turn.

His brother's love is there for the asking. He must open his eyes to its presence and accept the gift already offered him, but within the illusion, veiled and unseen. His brother's love shines forth seeking recognition. Let us not deny him that gift of giving. These are the lessons which will take endless teaching. Through your own demonstration of forgiveness toward the children with whom you work, as well as your gentle guidance as they counsel each other, you and they will find God's presence.

Use prayer and meditation as well as allegorical stories. The children will relate to the animals and their problems. Through the animals the children can become observers of their own experiences. *

Through forgiveness the world is saved from its illusions of fear and guilt. The children with whom you are working need the assurance that their world is not filled with malice and hate, fear and revenge. Through the outward expression of their inner light and love they will see their reflection in their brother. Each child needs the reassurance that only through his constant giving, not taking will he receive. Here is that very different but oh so rewarding lesson, directly opposite to the ego's interpretation: To give IS to receive. Show each child that as he gives so shall he receive the same in return. As he shows love to his brothers so shall he receive love in return. Conversely, as he shows fear to his brother so shall that be returned also.

This is a very easy lesson for the children to help illustrate. There isn't one instance of interpersonal relationships the children have been through that day or week which cannot be used to explain this concept. The arguments and bickering which seem to escalate and spiral between children are easily used as illustrations. Remember to emphasize the children's basic and usually unquestioning generosity for it is through the positive examples that the concept of forgiveness will be reinforced.

*(See Little Lamb, Part I)

Sharing, Not Bargaining

In all special relationships there is an element of bargaining. You see another as the answer to a need. You agree to give that person "love" in the hopes of receiving something in return. When your desires are not specifically met, you retract your "love." Now you extend fear and anger hoping that by making the other guilty they will return your "gifts; " and so they do, returning fear and guilt in turn to you.

Now is the time to show children that they must not bargain, but share. In bargaining the only exchange between brothers is fear and guilt, a heavy burden to carry. Through the sharing of God's love, without questioning or looking for a specific outcome, shall joy be felt.

Love is a glorious gift given to each of us, for it is truly the essence of God Himself. To share with another is simply the acknowledgment of that love which shines radiant and pure within us. God's gift of love remains with you. The tragedy is your blindness to it. Help open the eyes of the children with whom you work by opening your own. As you see the perfection in each of your students so shall the brightness within them be reflected to you in greater magnitude, shining away the dark places in all your hearts.

Miracles

The basis for the awakening process is within the miracle. it is through this illusion, sent by the Holy Spirit and used for Holy purpose, that you and the children will be aware of God.

Teach well the dynamics of miracles.

1. Recognize that a healing must take place.
2. Ask the Holy Spirit's guidance.
3. Listen. This is so important, for what good is asking if you refuse to listen.
4. Faithfully trust in the Holy Spirit's sure guidance. The healing has taken place. Hold fast to that belief and allow the Holy Spirit to use you, time and place according to His wise judgment. Faith is a key word. It is only through your faith in the Holy Spirit and the sure knowledge that miracles are natural that they will become apparent to you.

Your work is beginning. You, the teachers of young minds, listen well. Listen to your Self. Listen to the Self in each of your students. Listen for the Holy Spirit's sure guidance within all that you see, hear and do.

Miracles are your right to be shared and experienced with all your brothers. Miracles heal. Let the Holy Spirit heal you and your brothers simultaneously and heaven shall be yours now.

You are ready to use these concepts with your students. They will come to you for now you are ready to learn from them.

APPLICATION

Sequence of the material presented should follow a very carefully formulated pattern. The child-mind must be introduced to the concepts in small easily digestible doses. Beginning with awareness of self, in conjunction with the universe, he can begin to assimilate information showing his relationship to others and the individual relationship to the whole or God.

Once his position in the universal consciousness is determined he can then develop an understanding of the way he affects the world he perceives and the way he is affected only by his thoughts. This is crucial to his growing understanding of miracles. In all lessons, over and over, the concept of leaving judgment to the Holy Spirit should be emphasized.

Now that his place in the universe has been established and the effects of thought given application, he will be able to apply these concepts to his everyday life. We now have a budding teacher of God. How exhilarating! To be able to help mold spiritual growth is truly the work of saints.

Now that the pattern has been formed you will be ready to begin day to day lesson plans. Each lesson will be followed by a short prayer period. This will be the opportunity to introduce the actual workbook lessons. Use these lessons as the basis for your prayer segment. Help the children reach deeply within themselves for the answers to their problems. Within the heart the seeds of love lie dormant waiting for the blessed water of enlightenment.

Suggested Lesson Plan

1. Short discussion of the past week. This allows the children to be comfortable with each other.

2. Story, play, songs, puppets, film. This will be the presentation of the day's concept.

3. Discussion. Allow the children to express any and all feelings about the presentation. Guide the children toward the basic truth given.

4. Counseling. Help the children help themselves and each other through the practical application of the concept presented.

5. Prayer. Use this time to teach meditation based on the workbook lesson. Some preliminary explanation may be necessary, but the concept for the day should coincide with the prayer.

Suggested Questions and Sequence

Each of these suggested questions can form the basis for your teaching format. Expand on these even further as you wish. Allow the flow of ideas to expand your lessons rather than restrict them. This is a course in illumination. Do not stifle your growth or your students'.

1. Teach the oneness of the Son with the Father
   - Who are we?
   - How do we see ourselves as limited?
   - Why do we see ourselves as limited?
   - What is spirit?
   - Where does spirit live?

2. Reality vs. reality
   - What is real?
   - What things change?
   - How does thought affect how we see life?
   - How does thought affect our bodies?
   - Does love change?

3. Relinquishment of ties to ego
   - Begin counseling among students.
   - Open their thoughts to love, away from fear.
   - Listen for the Holy Spirit's instructions.

Give up judgment.

4. Special Relationship to Holy Relationship
   - Forgiveness. This should be stressed repeatedly.
   - Counseling among students.
   - Is love or fear expressed in a relationship?
   - How to shift from fear to love.

5. Oneness of the Sonship
   - Review and expand the concept of spirit.
   - How is brotherhood shown?
   - Can separation truly be a reality?

6. What are miracles?
   - When do miracles occur?
   - The natural quality of miracles.
   - The dynamics of miracles.

Little Lamb's

Cut and Color Projects

To be used whenever it seems like fun!

This Project Book is given to you for your pleasure. Inside you will find QUESTIONS, ANSWERS, and fun make-and-do PROJECTS.

Learning can open your mind and make you see things differently.

Learning helps you to grow, so you can help yourself and others.

Learning is a sharing experience, for it helps you have fun with others.

Learning never stops, but you do have a choice of what you want to learn:

Things that make you HAPPY,

or

Things that make you sad.

Which do you want to learn?

This Project Book will help answer your questions and help you feel HAPPY.

Now it's time to open to the first page and see what gifts Little Lamb has for you. . .

WHO AM I!

"You are my brother or sister. We are part of the same family. We have one Father Who loves all His children exactly the same.

Let's see how big our family is!

"See the sun and clouds? See the birds flying? See the tree and flowers on the next page?

. . .What else can you draw to show God's whole family? (Don't forget to draw yourself!)

HOW DO I SEE MYSELF?

Take a look at yourself in a mirror. What do you see? Are you short or are you tall? Is your hair dark or is it light? What color are your eyes?

See the mirror on the next page? Draw a picture of yourself in the mirror. Add your name in the box below.

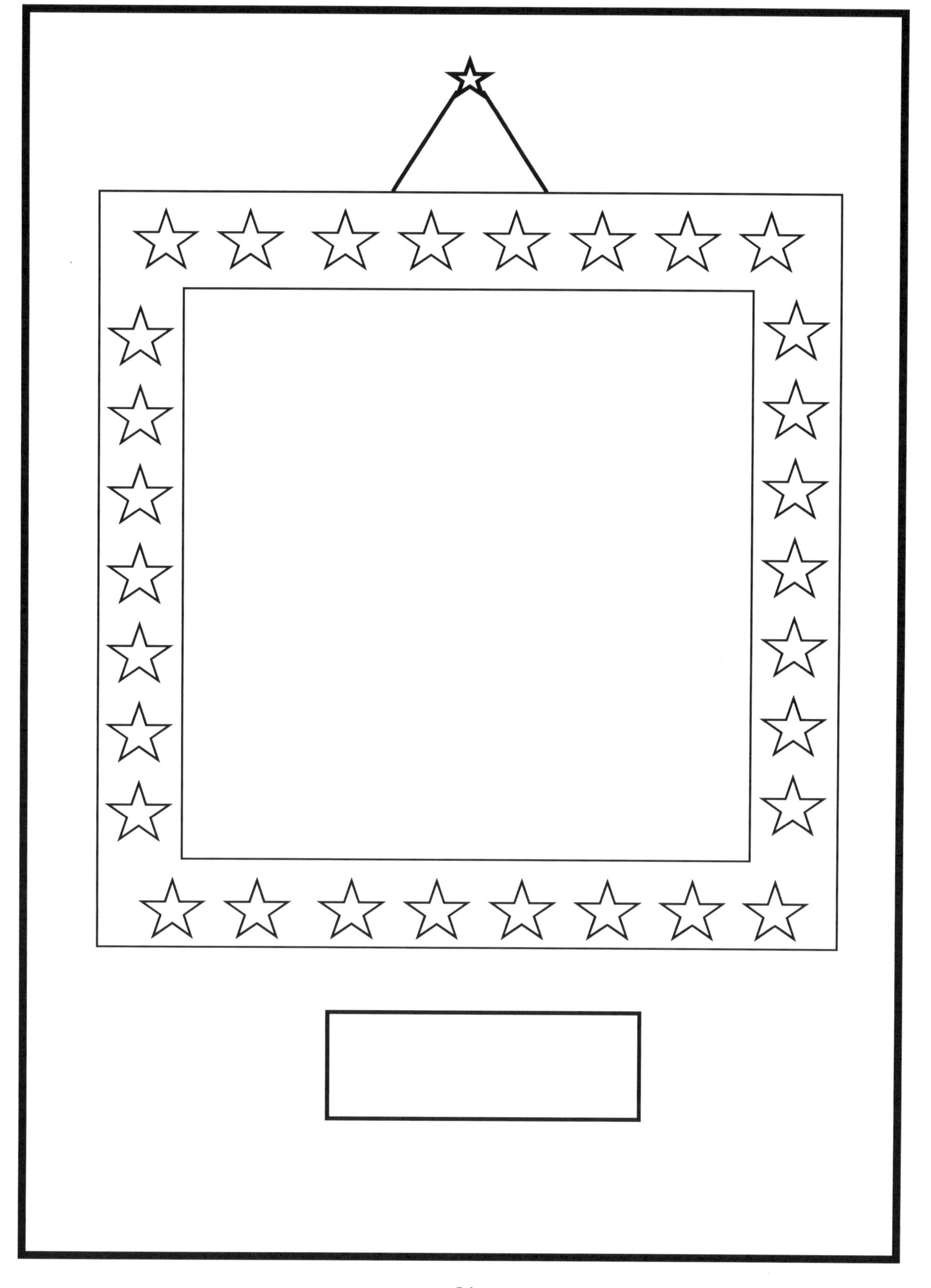

IS THIS REALLY ME?

Are you really only your body? Are you really only your hair, your arms, your muscles and bones? Is this all you really are? Or are you more than this? Of course! You are your feelings, too.

JOYFUL

Draw in the faces on the next page to fit the feelings written below.

Now circle the face and feeling you WOULD LIKE TO HAVE.

ANGRY
JOYFUL
SAD
HAPPY
WORRIED
LAUGHING

IF I AM MORE THAN MY BODY, THEN WHAT AM I?

You are a child of God. God does not have a body. He is only LOVE. He is SPIRIT.
You are His child and you are just like Him. So you are Love and you are Spirit. That is what you truly are!

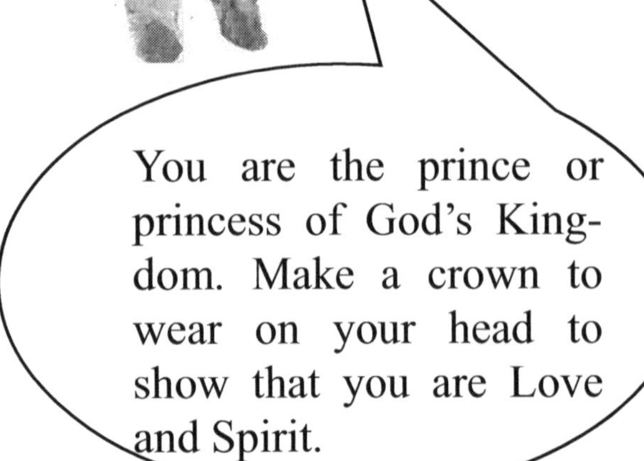

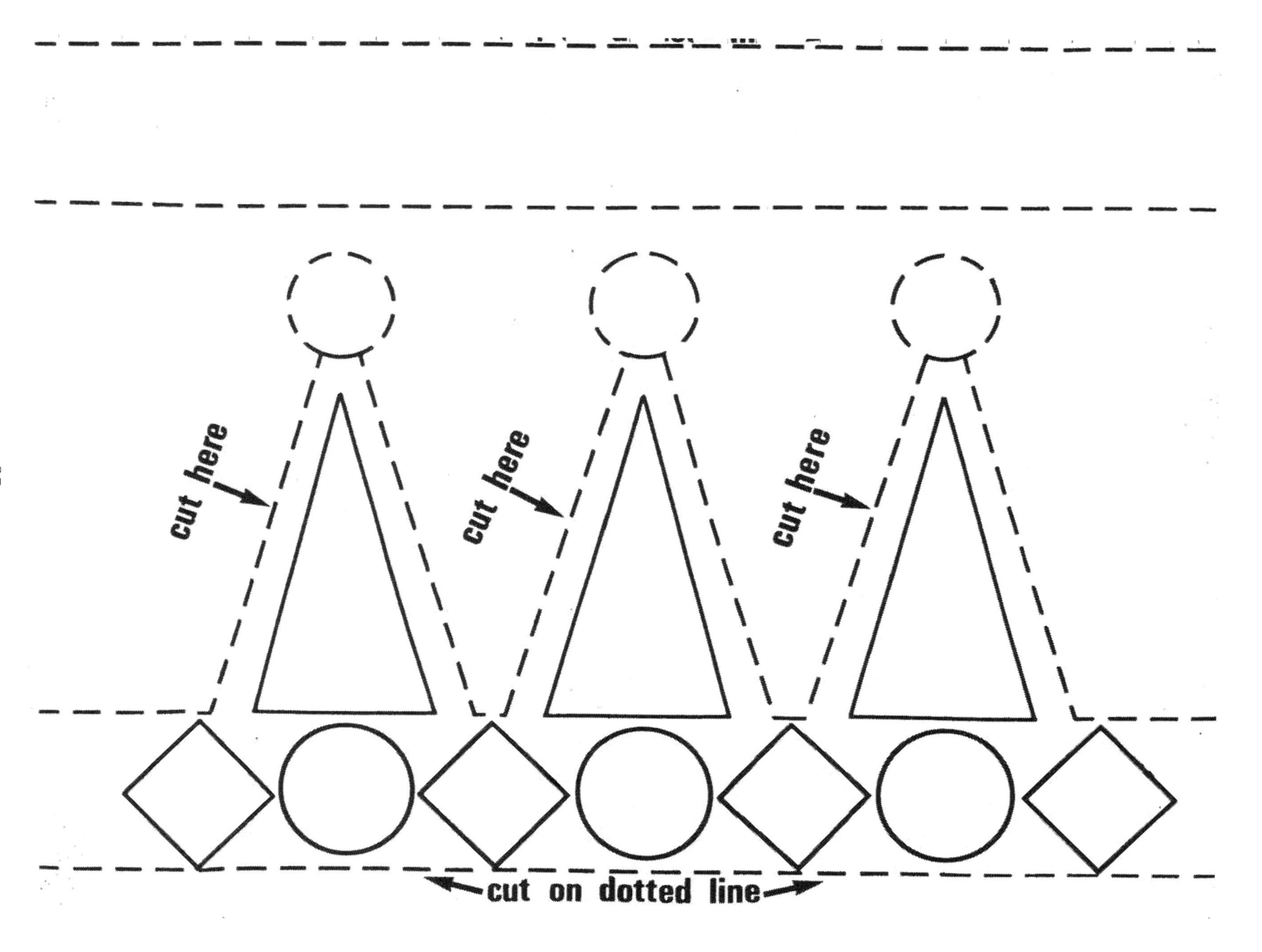
cut here
cut here
cut here
cut on dotted line

Here is a fun page. You can drawn anything you want here.

Here is a fun page. You can drawn anything you want here.

SINCE I AM SPIRIT, WHY DO I HAVE A BODY?

Your body helps you do things in this world., like nice things for others and also for yourself. You can use your body to remember that you are really Love and Spirit.

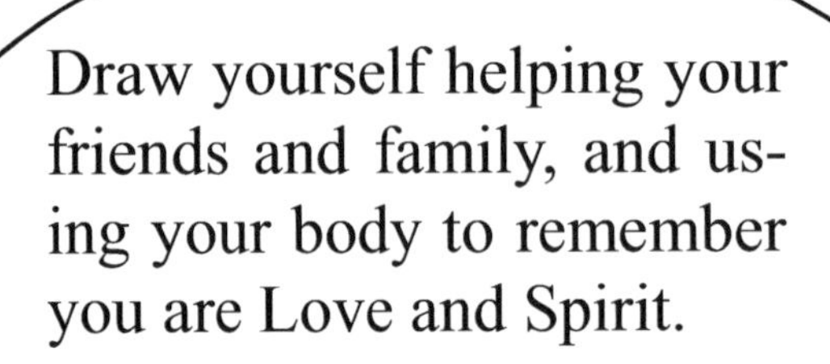

Draw yourself helping your friends and family, and using your body to remember you are Love and Spirit.

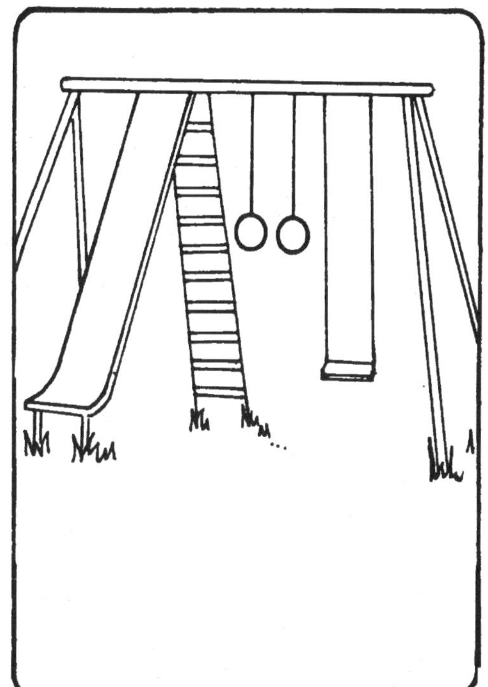

WHERE IS GOD'S HOME?

God lives forever in heaven. You are His Child and live there with Him. Where is heaven? Right here—right now because God's Home is shining in your heart!

Cut out these hearts. Trace them on aluminum foil. Cut out and paste the foil on the hearts. Now, pin a shining heart on your shirt. Heaven is shining in your heart. Make more shining hearts for your friends and family, too.

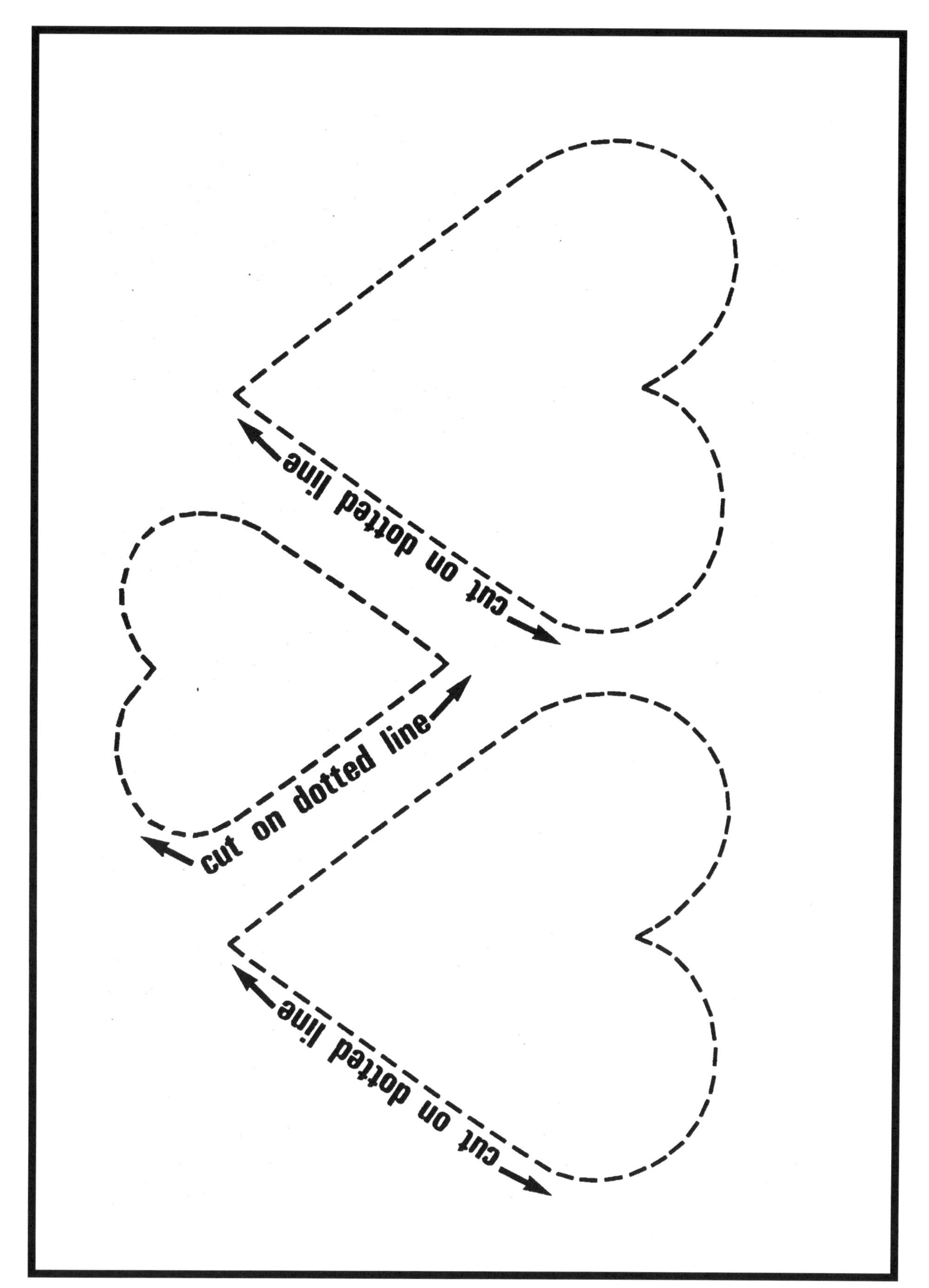
cut on dotted line
cut on dotted line
cut on dotted line

Here is a fun page. You can drawn anything you want here.

Here is a fun page. You can drawn anything you want here.

WHY DON'T I ALWAYS FEEL GOD'S LOVE?

Close your eyes tightly and you can believe you are alone even when your family is there. So, close your mind to loving thoughts and you will think God isn't there.

Cut out the whole heart. Cut out the two heart halves. Put paste on the whole heart just where it says. Put the two halves on top of the whole one. Now carefully fold the halves open and see what it says.

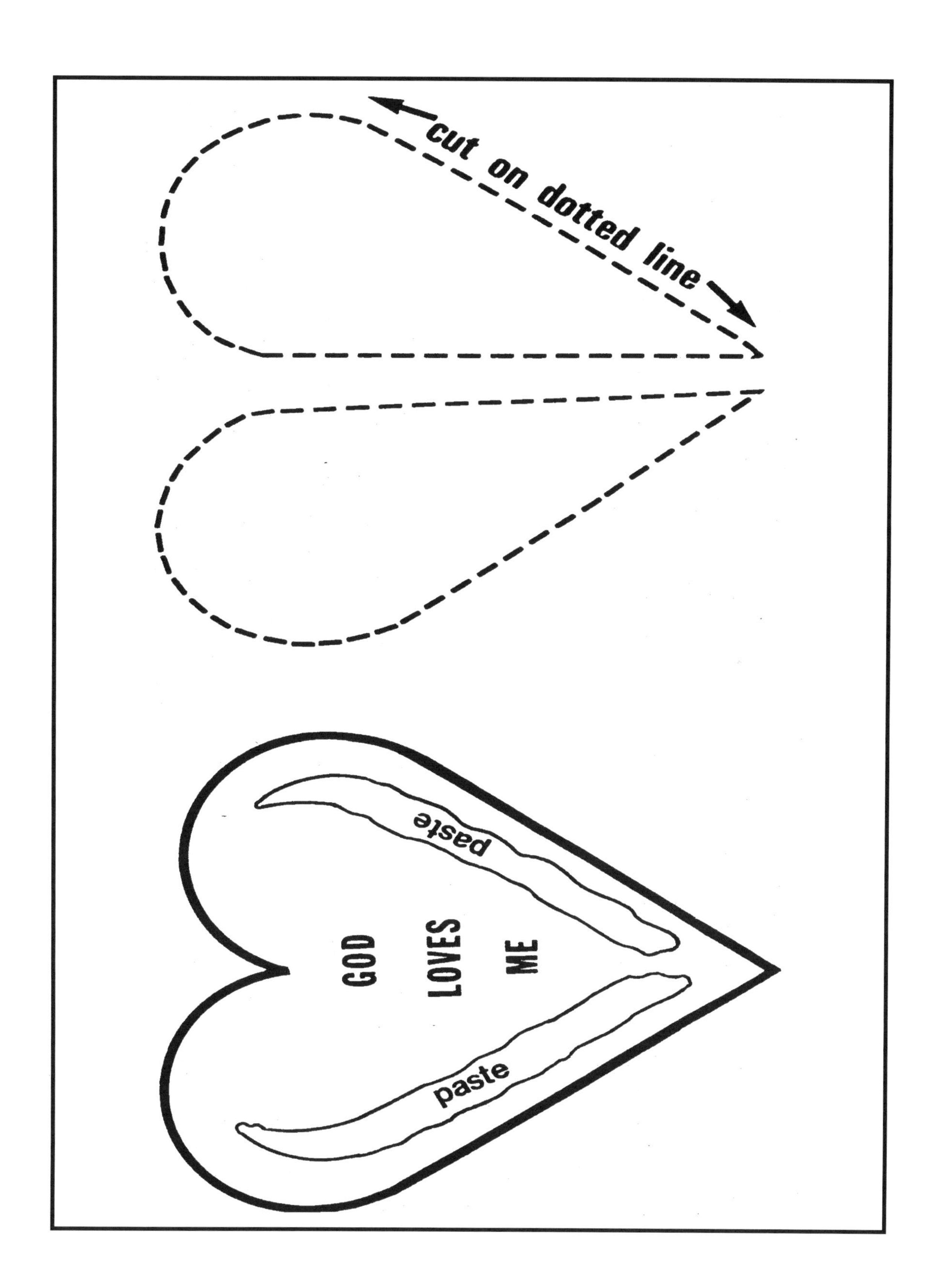
cut on dotted line
paste
GOD
LOVES
ME
paste

Here is a fun page. You can drawn anything you want here.

Here is a fun page. You can drawn anything you want here.

HOW CAN I HELP OTHERS BE HAPPY, TOO?

Smiling is a great way to say, “I like you and want you to be happy with me.” So share lots of smiles with everyone and help them feel happy. And, guess what? You will feel even happier!

Draw smiling faces in the boxes and see how much happier you are, too.

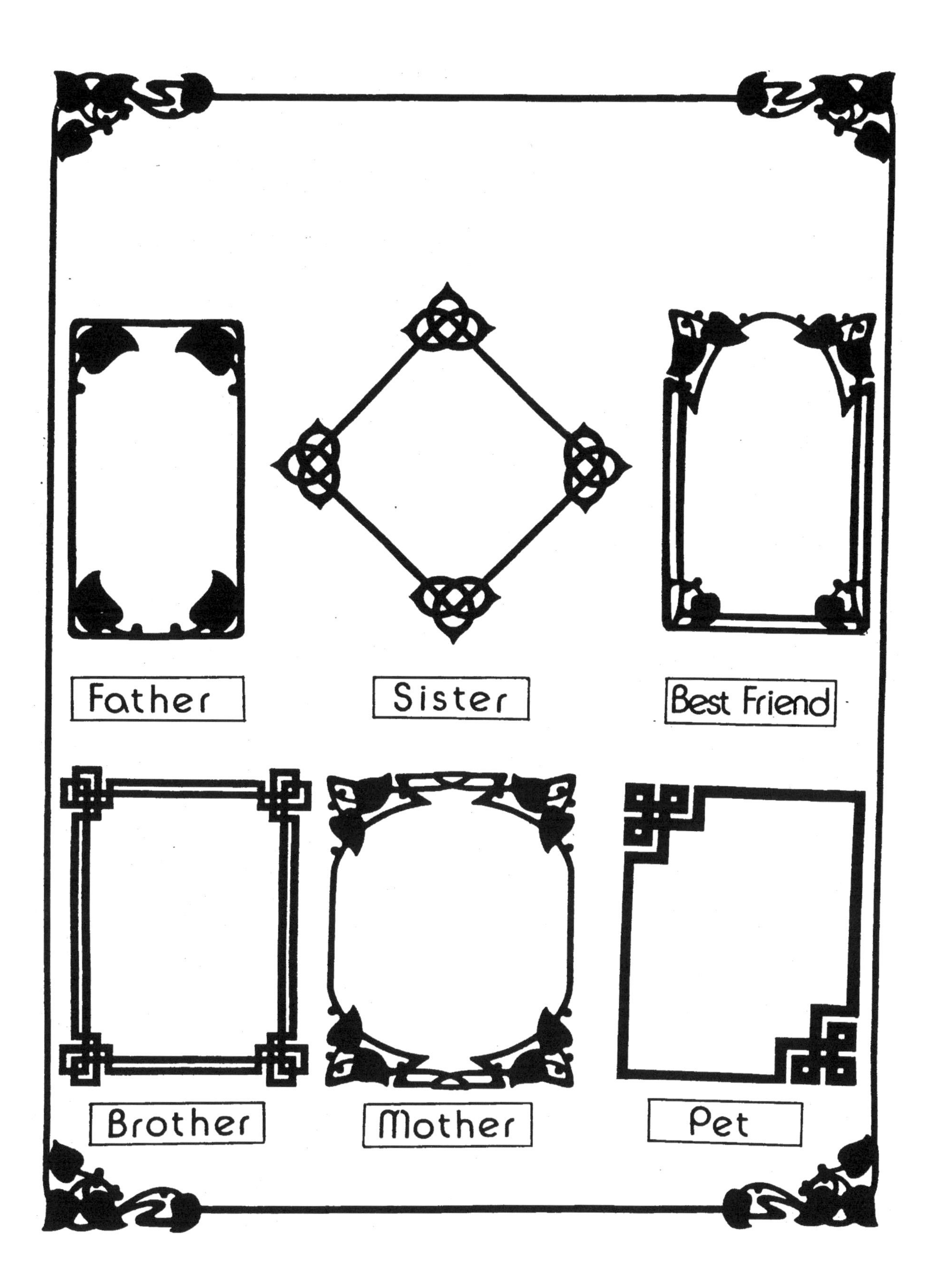
Father
Sister
Best Friend
Brother
Mother
Pet

I love you!

El Material
Para
Los Niños

Pequeño Corero
Las Fábulas de los Milagros
y
Libro de Ejercicios

Pequeño Corero

Las Fábulas de los Milagros

El Mundo de Nuestro Padre

El mundo de Dios estaba en todas partes y lo era todo. El mundo de Dios estaba lleno de Amor y belleza. El mundo de Dios estaba lleno con la música de la felicidad. Los burbujeantes arroyos reían felizmente. La Luz del sol bailaba y parpadeaba. Los árboles susurraban su satisfacción.

Pequeño Cordero estaba en paz en el mundo de su Padre. Había cálida luz solar, agua fresca para beber y verde hierba para comer. Todos los animales vivían en Amor y hermandad. Su Padre estaba en ellos y a su alrededor. Él les hablaba en sus corazones.

Un día, Dios llamó a Pequeño Cordero: "Pequeño Cordero, necesito tu ayuda".

"Señor Padre", contestó Pequeño Cordero, "¿cómo puedo ayudarte?".

Y su Padre dijo: "Pequeño Cordero, tú eres perfecto y amoroso, tal como son todos Mis niños. Y cuando ellos están despiertos en Mi mundo pueden ver su perfección, puesto que Yo los amo a todos y los he creado perfectos. Pero, a veces, Mis niños duermen, y cuando están dormidos sueñan, y en sus sueños olvidan Mi Amor. Olvidan que son perfectos. Olvidan a su Padre, quien siempre está con ellos y los ama.

"Tú, Pequeño Cordero, entiendes esto y puedes ver el Amor en todos tus hermanos. Ahora debes dormir y soñar. Sueña, Pequeño Cordero, pero en tus sueños recuérdame y ayuda a tus hermanos para que ellos también me recuerden. Enséñales que el mundo que creen ver es simplemente un sueño. Ayúdalos a despertar y a abrir sus ojos a Mi mundo Real, donde están el Amor y la felicidad".

Y Pequeño Cordero se llenó con el encanto y la paz del Amor de Dios. "Sí, Padre. Dormiré y soñaré. Pero recordaré que Tú estás siempre conmigo. Entraré en el mundo del sueño y ayudaré a todos mis hermanos a recordarte y a despertar a Tu mundo Real".

A medida que el sol se escondía suavemente detrás de los árboles, Pequeño Cordero se acurrucó cómodamente haciéndose un ovillo. La música de los pájaros e insectos sonaba dulcemente susurrando una canción de cuna, tranquilizando a Pequeño Cordero para ayudarle a dormir. Y en su corazón, oyó las palabras de su Padre: "Tú eres Mi Hijo, en quien me complazco. Tu trabajo ha comenzado. Sueña dulces sueños, Pequeño Cordero. Y en tus sueños despierta a Mis Niños para que recuerden Mi Amor por ellos".

Desde El Miedo al Amor

Pequeño Cordero abrió sus ojos lentamente. Cuidadosamente se puso de pie. "Aprende, disfruta y enseña. Tienes mucho que hacer", dijo la Voz de Dios en su corazón.

"Deprisa, deprisa Pequeño Cordero, necesitamos tu ayuda". En el sueño, Pequeño Cordero abrió sus ojos. Los animales del bosque estaban a su alrededor. Ratón corría de aquí para allá. Mapache se ocultó parcialmente tras un tronco de árbol cortado.

"Debes ayudarnos, Pequeño Cordero", dijo Ratón. El miedo mantenía crispados sus bigotes. "Hay algo horrible en el bosque y tú debes salvarnos". Mapache se escondió un poco más tras el tronco, esperando que nadie pudiera verlo.

"¿Habéis ido a ver lo que es?", preguntó Pequeño Cordero. "El miedo de vuestros corazones desaparecerá cuando sepáis qué es lo que os asusta".

Ratón miró a Mapache y se enojó crispando sus bigotes. Mapache, asustado, se escondió aún más detrás del tronco y dijo: "Tenemos demasiado miedo para ir a ver".

El corazón de Pequeño Cordero se abrió hacia sus amigos. Él sabía que debía descubrir lo que se escondía en la oscuridad del bosque porque el miedo desaparece a la luz del Amor... y se fue, sin miedo, lleno del Amor de su Padre.

Como empezaba a oscurecer, Pequeño Cordero se adentró en el bosque. Sus amigos estaban lejos, detrás de él. Se adentró más y más profundamente. La oscuridad le cubrió y se sintió solo. Había olvidado que su Padre estaría siempre con él.

Separado de sus amigos en un lugar del bosque que no conocía, Pequeño Cordero tuvo miedo. El chasquido de una rama cerca de él le hizo saltar de miedo. Ahora parecía estar rodeado de susurros y crujidos. Su corazón latía fuertemente en su pecho.

"¡Oh!, ¿por qué estoy aquí?". Y tan pronto como hubo hecho la pregunta, la respuesta llegó. Suave y amablemente, las palabras surgieron de su corazón. "Estás en el mundo del sueño, Pequeño Cordero, y viniste para ayudar a tus amigos a despertar, porque tú los amas como yo te amo a ti".

Entonces, Pequeño Cordero supo que no estaba solo, pues su Padre estaba con él. El miedo abandonó a Pequeño Cordero, y en su lugar llegó la paz y la felicidad porque pudo sentir el Amor de su Padre. Por primera vez, Pequeño Cordero miró hacia arriba y vio la luna brillando a través de los árboles. Tan intensamente brillaba que podía ver a su alrededor como si fuese de día. Y allí, escondiéndose tras un gran arbusto, había un animal. Su piel era de color amarillo dorado. Una gran melena de pelo rodeaba su cara. Era un león.

"Hola León", le dijo Pequeño Cordero. Según habló, vio lágrimas cayendo de los ojos del León. Amablemente, Pequeño Cordero preguntó: "¿Puedo ayudarte?".

"¡Estoy tan solo y asustado! Cada vez que me acerco a saludar a alguien, se aleja corriendo".

Pequeño Cordero sonrió. Entonces esto era lo que Ratón y Mapache temían. Sólo era un león, y estaba solo y asustado, igual que ellos. "Ven, no temas. Seamos amigos, y yo te ayudaré a conocer a los amigos que estás buscando".

Cuando Pequeño Cordero y León salieron del bosque, Ratón, con los bigotes crispados, se escondió tras una roca. Mapache se escabulló bajo un helecho, con los ojos muy abiertos y asustados.

"Venid, no os asustéis", llamó Pequeño Cordero a sus amigos. "León estaba solo en el bosque y necesita nuestra amistad tanto como nosotros la suya. Venid y conoced lo que os asustaba, ya que él es igual que vosotros. Solo y asustado busca vuestra amistad. ¿Podéis decirle que no?".

Y así, Ratón y Mapache se acercaron lentamente. A medida que el miedo de los animales comenzó a desaparecer fue reemplazado por la amistad y el Amor.

Pequeño Cordero pudo oír la voz de su Padre hablar a todos ellos en sus corazones: "Hoy vosotros habéis elegido el Amor en lugar del miedo, pues en ausencia del miedo sólo puede haber Amor".

Ratón dijo: "Gracias, Pequeño Cordero, por enseñarnos a ver más allá del miedo el Amor que siempre está ahí, esperando a que nosotros nos acerquemos y lo aceptemos". Entonces, Ratón alargó su mano y cogió la pata de León. El miedo había desaparecido y sólo reinaba el Amor entre ellos.

La Voz de Nuestro Padre

Pequeño Cordero recordó las palabras de su Padre. Él se adentraría en el mundo del sueño y despertaría a todos aquellos que estuviesen dormidos y hubiesen olvidado el mundo de su Padre. La oscuridad, tan suave como una manta, cubría a Pequeño Cordero, y en su sueño empezó a soñar. Y en el sueño, se encontró en un camino del bosque.

Ardilla Gris corría apresuradamente de un lado a otro bajo un gran árbol cuyas hojas eran naranja brillante.

"Hola, Ardilla Gris. ¿Cómo estás en este estupendo día?", preguntó Pequeño Cordero.

"¡Fatal, fatal! Así es como estoy en este estupendo día de otoño. Pronto llegará la helada y, después, la nieve. La nieve cubrirá todas las nueces y semillas. ¿Qué comeré entonces? ¡Oh cielos!, ¿qué haré?" ...Y la ardilla se alejó corriendo.

Pequeño Cordero siguió bajando por el camino del bosque y allí se encontró a Oso. "Hola Oso. ¿Cómo estás en este estupendo día?", preguntó Pequeño Cordero.

Oso bajó la mirada tristemente hacia Pequeño Cordero y suspiró: "El largo invierno se acerca y yo soy un gran oso. Siempre estoy hambriento. ¿Cómo podré vivir durante el invierno cuando la nieve llegue y las abejas dejen de producir miel para que yo coma?". Oso caminó despacio entre los árboles del bosque suspirando profundamente para sí mismo.

De nuevo, Pequeño Cordero descendió un poco más por el sendero. Sobre su cabeza volaba una bandada de gansos agitando sus alas ruidosamente. "¿A dónde vais en este estupendo día?", preguntó Pequeño Cordero.

"¿A dónde? ¡Oh! ¿Dónde podemos ir?", preguntó el ganso mayor. "Pronto llegará el invierno y los lagos se helarán y los árboles se cubrirán de nieve. ¿Dónde viviremos sin helarnos?"... Y los gansos se fueron volando y graznando tristemente.

Pequeño Cordero se sentó a un lado del camino. Estaba preocupado por los problemas de sus amigos. Sabía que debía ayudarles, pero ¿cómo? Entonces, Pequeño Cordero cerró sus ojos y en su corazón pidió la ayuda de su Padre. "Padre, mis amigos están preocupados y asustados. Necesitan Tu ayuda. ¿Qué puedo hacer?".

A través de la bruma del sueño, la Voz de su Padre le contestó: "Di a tus amigos, Pequeño Cordero, que Yo escucharé sus preguntas y les contestaré. Todo lo que deben hacer es preguntar y, entonces, abrirse a escuchar Mi respuesta en sus corazones. Yo amo a todos Mis niños y siempre estoy aquí para ayudarles".

Y así, Pequeño Cordero reunió a todos los animales y les dijo: "Nuestro Padre, Quien siempre está con nosotros, os ayudará. Todo lo que debéis hacer es cerrar vuestros ojos, pedir Su ayuda y escuchar vuestros corazones. Él contestará".

Ardilla Gris cerró sus ojos y dijo: "Padre, estoy preocupada. Pronto la nieve cubrirá las nueces y semillas. ¿Cómo comeré?". Ardilla Gris se sentó tranquilamente y escuchó su corazón.

congelados y los árboles llenos de nieve?". Entonces, el ganso se sentó en silencio y escuchó su corazón.

"No te preocupes, Ganso", le dijo la Voz de su Padre. "Toma tu bandada y vuela lejos hacia el sur. Allí, el invierno será cálido y encontrarás lagos para nadar y ramas frondosas para posarse".

"Gracias, Padre. Ahora sé lo que debo hacer". Y la bandada se fue volando hacia el sur.

Pequeño Cordero sonrió. Había ayudado a sus amigos. Ahora sabían que sólo debían preguntar y después abrirse a escuchar la Voz amorosa de su Padre, porque en el Amor de su Padre estaba la respuesta a todas sus preguntas.

"Hoy has hecho bien, Hijo mío", le dijo la Voz de su Padre. Pequeño Cordero abrió sus ojos. Había estado soñando y ahora se despertaba en el mundo de Dios. Pequeño Cordero era feliz.

Todos Somos Hijos de Nuestro Padre

Pequeño Cordero estaba en el mundo del sueño. Se encontraba con todos los animales del bosque. Las brisas cálidas de la tarde les rozaban suavemente mientras escuchaban sentados a Pequeño Cordero.

La Señorita Conejo avanzó con timidez y preguntó delicadamente a Pequeño Cordero: "Tú nos dices que todos somos hermanos y hermanas, pero no entiendo. Yo tengo largas orejas, un cuerpo cubierto de suave pelo y fuertes patas para brincar con ellas. El Señor y la Señora Cisne tienen largos cuellos, plumas, alas para volar y pies palmeados para nadar. ¿Cómo podemos ser hermanas y hermanos?".

Entonces, Búho dijo en voz alta: "Sí, Pequeño Cordero, ¿cómo puedo ser yo hermano de la Señorita Cierva? Yo duermo todo el día y estoy despierto toda la noche, y ella duerme toda la noche y está despierta de día".

Oso habló fuertemente, con su profunda voz: "Mira lo grande que soy y lo pequeño que es Ratón. ¿Podríamos ser hermanos?".

Pequeño Cordero sonrió amorosamente a sus amigos y dijo a la Señorita Conejo: "¿Cómo son tu madre y tu padre?".

La Señorita Conejo dijo: "¡Pues bueno, ellos tienen largas orejas, un cuerpo velludo y patas fuertes como yo!".

"Dime, Búho", preguntó Pequeño Cordero, "¿cómo son tus padres?".

Búho pensó durante un instante y dijo: "Sabes, ellos duermen todo el día y están despiertos de noche, igual que yo".

A continuación, Pequeño Cordero se dirigió hacia Oso y dijo: "Tu padre debe ser grande, igual que tú". Y Oso, moviendo su cabeza, dijo: "Sí".

"Todos vosotros sois hijos de vuestros padres. Os pare-

céis a ellos y actuáis como ellos. Ahora decidme: ¿Quién es el Padre de todos y de todo?".

Todos los animales sonrieron y dijeron juntos: "Dios es el Padre de todos y de todo".

"Ahora decidme cómo es Dios nuestro Padre".

Oso dijo en voz alta: "Él es todopoderoso".

Búho dijo pensativo: "Él es muy sabio y lo sabe todo".

La Señorita Conejo dijo ruborizada y discreta: "Él es nuestro Padre y nos ama".

Pequeño Cordero preguntó a sus amigos: "¿Podéis ver a Dios nuestro Padre?".

La Señorita Cierva miró hacia arriba y dijo: "Dios está en nuestros corazones. Él no es algo que VES, Dios es Amor, y eso es algo que sólo puedes SENTIR".

Entonces, Pequeño Cordero miró a todos sus amigos y dijo: "Dios nuestro padre es poderoso, sabio y amoroso. Él está siempre en nuestros corazones dispuesto a ayudarnos. Ahora pensad por un instante. Vosotros sois los hijos de vuestros padres y, según son vuestros padres, así sois vosotros. Si Dios está en todos vuestros corazones, entonces vosotros debéis también estar en todos los de vuestros hermanos y hermanas. Si Dios está siempre dispuesto a ayudarnos y amarnos, entonces nosotros estamos siempre dispuestos a ayudarnos y amarnos mutuamente, ya que Dios es nuestro Padre, y nosotros somos como Él".

Los ojos de Búho se iluminaron y dijo: "Ahora entiendo. Nuestros cuerpos son sólo disfraces que nos ponemos para divertirnos. Nos ayudan a realizar nuestros trabajos. Pero es lo que está dentro lo que es real. Ahí es donde Dios está. Y donde Dios nuestro Padre está, ahí están también nuestros hermanos y hermanas. Están en nuestros corazones siempre".

Pequeño Cordero sonrió, y todos los animales sonrieron entre ellos. En sus corazones podían oír la Voz de su Padre diciendo: "Todos vosotros sois Mis Hijos: poderosos, sabios y siempre amorosos, porque Yo os he hecho así".

Y mientras brillaba la suave luz de la luna sobre ellos, pudieron sentir en sus corazones que eran realmente hermanos y hermanas. Eran uno.

El Perdón

Pequeño Cordero cerró sus ojos y rápidamente se quedó dormido. Debía entrar en el sueño de nuevo, ya que tenía más trabajo que hacer.

Dos ardillas listadas estaban haciendo un ruido horrible en un claro del bosque repleto de hierba. Estaban parloteando enfadadas. Comenzaron a volar trocitos de hierba a medida que las dos empezaron a pellizcarse y arañarse una a otra.

"Tú siempre encuentras las nueces mayores y nunca me dejas a mí ninguna", chillaba Pequeña Ardilla.

"Tienes razón", gritaba contestando la otra.

"Siempre que encuentro algunas nueces tú te escabulles con ellas". Y de nuevo comenzaron a pelearse. Trocitos de pelo y hierba volaban por el aire.

Pequeño Cordero se acercó a ellas y les dijo: "Hermanas mías, ¿qué puede haberos enfadado tanto?".

Gran Ardilla dejó de pellizcar a Pequeña Ardilla y dijo: "Cada día me levanto muy temprano y trabajo duro recogiendo nueces para comer, y cada noche, cuando estoy profundamente dormida, ella viene y me las roba. Esto no es justo".

Pequeña Ardilla levantó su mirada hacia Pequeño Cordero y, con lágrimas de dolor y enfado en sus ojos, dijo: "Gran Ardilla nunca comparte sus nueces conmigo. Cada día salimos a buscar nueces para comer y cada día ella encuentra muchas más y mayores. Yo soy mucho más pequeña que ella. No puedo correr tan rápido; por tanto, no puedo encontrarlas primero. No soy tan fuerte y no puedo cargar tantas como ella. Siempre tengo hambre y nunca tengo suficiente para comer. Sin embargo, ella siempre tiene de

sobra. Esto no es justo. Así que, cuando Gran Ardilla no está mirando, le robo algunas de sus nueces para mí".

Pequeño Cordero miró a ambas ardillas. Podía ver el miedo que tenían en sus corazones. Pudo ver que este miedo era el que las estaba haciendo enfadarse la una con la otra.

Pequeño Cordero dijo: "Hermanas, ambas estabais asustadas por si no teníais suficiente para comer. Ambas fuisteis egoístas y olvidasteis mirar a vuestra hermana con Amor. Sentíais miedo y enfado y le disteis eso a vuestra hermana, y eso es lo que ella os devolvió. Ahora vamos a tratar de ver sólo el bien y el Amor en el otro, y seguro que eso es lo que recibiréis de vuelta".

Gran Ardilla miró a la pequeña y dijo: "Si tú estabas siempre hambrienta y yo siempre tenía suficiente comida, ¿por qué nunca me pediste algunas nueces? Seguro que te las hubiera dado".

Pequeña Ardilla miró a la grande y dijo: "Temía que no me dieses ninguna. Tú siempre parecías estar tan enfadada conmigo..."

"Sí, yo estaba enfadada porque pensaba que tú eras una ladrona. Pero ahora puedo ver que simplemente estabas hambrienta y asustada, asustada por si no tenías suficiente que comer y temerosa de mí". Ambas ardillas se miraron con nuevos ojos.

"Ciertamente", dijo Pequeño Cordero, "el enfado sólo viene del miedo, y si tan sólo miráis y escucháis a vuestra hermana con Amor, el miedo y, por lo tanto, el enfado, desaparecerán".

"A partir de ahora", dijo Gran Ardilla, "buscaremos nueces juntas. Tú puedes ayudarme a encontrarlas, y yo puedo ayudarte a cargarlas."

"Entonces, podremos compartirlas", dijo Pequeña Ardilla... Y se fueron corriendo juntas, felices de ser amigas y no enemigas.

Pequeño Cordero sonrió, ya que podía oír la Voz de su Padre en su corazón diciendo: "Tus hermanas se perdonaron mutuamente porque vieron la verdad: 'El enfado viene del miedo, y el miedo desaparece cuando se comparte el Amor'".

Con aquello, Pequeño Cordero abrió sus ojos y la bruma del sueño se aclaró. Había vuelto al mundo del Amor, de la paz y de la felicidad de su Padre.

El Elección

Pequeño Cordero se adentró de nuevo en el mundo del sueño. Su trabajo no estaría terminado mientras sus hermanos continuaran olvidando el mundo Real de Dios.

Pequeño Cordero y Castor caminaban juntos por el bosque. El sol brillaba intensamente a través de los árboles.

"El sol está muy brillante", dijo Castor. Podía sentir el calor del sol sobre su cabeza y pensó: "El sol está siempre muy caliente. Cuando estoy acalorado me siento cansado, y cuando estoy cansado me siento malhumorado. El sol está demasiado caliente".

Mientras Castor tenía sus pensamientos, Pequeño Cordero estaba pensando también: ¡"Qué maravillosamente cálido y agradable es el sol. Mira qué brillante y precioso hace que se vea el bosque! Gracias, Padre, por dejarme ver la belleza del sol".

Pequeño Cordero y Castor continuaron bajando el camino del bosque. Pronto estuvieron hambrientos y comenzaron a buscar algo para comer. Castor pensó: "Cada vez que estoy hambriento, debo buscar comida para comer. Debo buscar raíces escarbando en la sucia tierra. Debo trabajar siempre y cuando trabajo me siento cansado y cuando estoy cansado me siento malhumorado".

Pequeño Cordero también pensaba: "Mira toda esa bonita y verde hierba para comer. Mira todas esas raíces en el suelo para que mi amigo coma. ¡Qué maravilloso es Dios, Quien nos da todo lo que necesitamos! Gracias, Padre".

Después de comer, los amigos se sintieron cansados y decidieron descansar. Mientras Castor estaba tumbado en el suelo, pensó: "Escucha todos esos insectos zumbando. Escucha todos esos pájaros gorjeando. ¡Qué ruido tan horrible! ¿Cómo podré descansar si tengo que escuchar este alboroto?".

Pequeño Cordero también estaba tumbado para descansar y pensó: "Escucha a mis hermanos, los insectos, zumbando. Escucha a mis hermanos, los pájaros, gorjeando. ¡Qué preciosas son las canciones de la vida! Gracias, Padre, por enviarme una canción de cuna tan maravillosa".

Más tarde, Pequeño Cordero y Castor encontraron a otro castor junto a un arroyo.

"Por favor, ayudadme", rogó el otro castor. "Este tronco es muy grande para subirlo yo solo, y debo ponerlo en el arroyo para poder construir mi casa".

Mientras Pequeño Cordero y Castor ayudaban a su hermano a subir el tronco, Castor pensó: "Mira todo este trabajo que debo hacer ahora. El tronco me está ensuciando el pelaje, y el agua del arroyo me está dejando húmedo y frío; y cuando estoy sucio, húmedo y frío me siento malhumorado".

Pequeño Cordero también pensaba mientras ayudaba a su hermano: "¡Qué fresca está el agua y cómo limpia la suciedad de mi lana! ¡Qué bonito es ayudar a mi hermano! Gracias, Padre, por darme esta oportunidad de ayudar a un amigo y por darme el regalo de la sonrisa de agradecimiento de mi amigo".

Más avanzada la tarde, Castor oyó a Pequeño Cordero diciendo: "Gracias, Padre, por un día tan hermoso y feliz".

"¿Cómo puedes decir que este día ha sido hermoso y feliz?", exclamó Castor. "El sol estaba muy caliente. Fue duro encontrar comida para comer. El ruido de los pájaros e insectos me mantuvo despierto y me quedé sucio, húmedo y frío levantando el tronco".

"Pero, ¿no te das cuenta de que así es como tú decidiste ver el día?", dijo Pequeño Cordero. "Escucha cómo vi yo el día: 'El sol era cálido y hermoso; la hierba, dulce y abundante. Los pájaros me cantaron una canción de cuna, y nuestro hermano nos dio el regalo de su amorosa sonrisa...' Por todo ello estoy muy agradecido".

Los ojos de Castor comenzaron a iluminarse mientras decía: "¿Sabes, Pequeño Cordero?, no se trata de lo que hice hoy, sino de cómo decidí verlo. Elegí ver sólo infelicidad en todo lo que hicimos y me sentí malhumorado e infeliz. Tú elegiste ver sólo felicidad en todo lo que hicimos y te sentiste feliz".

"Ahora lo ves", dijo Pequeño Cordero sonriendo, "tú elegiste entre ser feliz o no serlo. Dios, nuestro Padre, nos da solamente Amor y bondad. Está en nuestras manos decidir si queremos ver ese Amor y esa bondad".

Según Castor miró a su alrededor, vio las estrellas brillando y sintió la brisa cálida de la noche tan suave como una manta sobre su pelaje y dijo: "Gracias, Padre, por esta bella noche". Entonces, Castor y Pequeño Cordero sonrieron.

La Felicidad

Pequeño Cordero atravesó la niebla del sueño. Sus hermanos le estaban esperando. Tenían preguntas que hacerle.

Pequeño Cordero se sentó en el centro del círculo. Todos sus hermanos, que vivían en el bosque, se sentaron a su alrededor y se dispusieron a escuchar.

"Pequeño Cordero", dijo uno de los animales, "háblanos sobre la felicidad".

Pequeño Cordero miró a todos sus amigos y sonrió: "Primero, dejadme preguntaros qué pensáis que es la felicidad".

Ardilla Gris miró a Pequeño Cordero y dijo: "La felicidad es tener montones y montones de semillas y nueces. Cuando tenga todas las semillas y nueces del mundo, entonces seré feliz".

"¿Eres feliz ahora?", preguntó Pequeño Cordero.

"No", dijo Ardilla Gris. "Pero lo seré cuando consiga todas las semillas y las nueces de este mundo".

Mamá Petirrojo, con lágrimas en los ojos, dijo: "Yo acabo de perder la felicidad. El verano pasado todos mis bebés estaban conmigo y yo les ayudaba a crecer grandes y fuertes. Ahora se han ido para tener sus propias familias, y con ellos se fue mi felicidad".

"¿Eres feliz ahora?", preguntó Pequeño Cordero.

"No", dijo Mamá Petirrojo. "Cuando mis niños estaban conmigo yo tenía felicidad, pero ahora se han ido y mi felicidad se ha ido también".

Rata habló a continuación. En sus patas mantenía todas las cosas extrañas que había encontrado ese día: una piedra, una bellota y una lata de hojalata. "Yo soy feliz cuando tengo conmigo todas las cosas que encuentro. Me llevó mucho tiempo encontrar estas cosas. No dejaré que nadie me las quite. Mientras las tengo, soy feliz".

"¿Eres feliz ahora?", preguntó Pequeño Cordero.

"Ahora soy feliz porque tengo todas mis cosas. Pero tengo miedo a perderlas". Y, así, Rata se sentó aferrándose a sus cosas, temerosa de perder su felicidad.

Pequeño Cordero miró a sus amigos y dijo: "Ardilla Gris no

es feliz ahora porque no ha encontrado aún la felicidad. Mamá Petirrojo no es feliz ahora porque acaba de perder su felicidad. Rata piensa que es feliz porque tiene todas sus cosas, pero está temerosa de perderlas; por tanto, si está temerosa, ¿puede realmente ser feliz?

Y Rata dijo: "Reconozco que no soy realmente feliz porque temo perder esas cosas que pensé que eran la felicidad. Dinos, Pequeño Cordero, ¿cómo podemos ser felices ahora?".

Pequeño Cordero sonrió a sus hermanos y dijo: "La felicidad no es algo o alguien o algún lugar. La felicidad simplemente está dentro de nosotros. Cuando sientes el Amor de Dios en tu corazón, te sientes feliz. Cuando compartes el Amor de Dios con todos tus hermanos, te sientes feliz, y cuando te sientes feliz por dentro, tu felicidad ilumina a todos los que te encuentras. Cuando te sientes feliz internamente, no importa con quién estés, dónde estés o lo que tengas. Estarás feliz porque llevas contigo la felicidad donde quiera que tú vas".

"¿Eres feliz ahora, Ardilla?", preguntó Pequeño Cordero.

"Sí, soy feliz. No son las nueces y semillas las que me hacen feliz. Soy sólo yo", dijo Ardilla.

"¿Eres feliz ahora, Mamá Petirrojo?", preguntó Pequeño Cordero.

"Sí, soy feliz, porque amo a mis hijos tanto si están conmigo como si no", dijo Mamá Petirrojo.

"¿Eres feliz ahora, Rata?", preguntó Pequeño Cordero.

"Sí, soy feliz, porque si estoy feliz dentro de mí no importa si tengo mis cosas o las pierdo, seguiré siendo feliz".

...Y tal cual estaban todos sentados en el círculo, sintieron el Amor de Dios en ellos y a su alrededor y fueron todos muy felices.

El Amor

Pequeño Cordero se adentró en la niebla del sueño y fue a dar a un encantador estanque. Dos cisnes comenzaron a nadar hacia él.

"Hola, Pequeño Cordero", dijo el Señor Cisne. "Me gustaría que conocieses a mi nueva esposa, a la que amo mucho". La Señora Cisne sonrió dulcemente a Pequeño Cordero.

"Hola, Señor y Señora Cisne", dijo Pequeño Cordero. "Parecéis muy felices juntos".

"Sí, somos felices", dijo el cisne, "porque nos amamos mutuamente".

Pequeño Cordero sonrió a sus amigos y preguntó: "¿Podéis decirme por qué os amáis el uno al otro?"

El Señor Cisne rió y dijo: "Eso es fácil porque ¡mi mujer es tan bonita!" Y la Señora Cisne dijo: "¡Es porque él es tan guapo!".

"Entonces, decidme", preguntó Pequeño Cordero. "Si tu mujer perdiese su belleza y tu marido se volviese feo, ¿os amaríais aún el uno al otro?".

Los cisnes se sonrieron mutuamente y dijeron: "Sí, aún nos amaríamos muchísimo".

"Entonces, decidme otra vez", preguntó Pequeño Cordero. "¿Por qué os amáis el uno al otro?".

El Señor Cisne pensó por un momento y dijo: "Yo sé que si necesito ayuda mi mujer estará ahí para ayudarme, y ése es el motivo por el que la amo". La Señora Cisne asintió con la cabeza, de acuerdo con su marido.

Pequeño Cordero preguntó: "Si tu mujer no pudiese estar ahí cuando tú la necesitases, ¿aún la amarías?"

"Sí, la amaría incluso si ella no pudiese estar ahí para ayudarme". Y la Señora Cisne sonrió a su marido.

"Entonces, decidme otra vez", preguntó Pequeño Cordero, "¿por qué os amáis el uno al otro?".

El Señor Cisne pensó otra vez y dijo: "Ella será una buena madre para nuestros hijos". A su vez, la Señora Cisne dijo: "Él será un buen padre para nuestros hijos".

Pequeño Cordero miró a sus amigos y preguntó: "¿Y qué pasaría si no tuvieseis ningún hijo?, ¿os amaríais aún el uno al otro?".

Los dos cisnes se miraron el uno al otro y dijeron juntos: "Si, aún así nos amaríamos muchísimo. Pero dinos, Pequeño Cordero, si nos amásemos incluso aunque fuéramos feos o no pudiésemos ayudarnos mutuamente o no pudiéramos tener hijos, entonces, ¿por qué nos amaríamos tanto?"

"Vosotros no os amáis DEBIDO A ninguna razón. El Amor es un regalo precioso dado por Dios a todos Sus hijos. Cuando sentimos el Amor de Dios en nosotros y a nuestro alrededor, podemos dar ese Amor a todos nuestros hermanos y hermanas. Vosotros habéis decidido sentir y disfrutar el Amor de Dios juntos. Disfrutad el regalo de Amor de Dios. Compartir es la parte más bonita de cualquier regalo".

Y según Pequeño Cordero les dijo adiós, los dos cisnes se fueron nadando felizmente. En su corazón, Pequeño Cordero podía oír la Voz de Dios: "Mientras Mis Hijos recuerden el Amor que yo doy a cada uno de ellos, tendrán siempre Amor para dar y compartir".

El Juicio

León estaba esperando a Pequeño Cordero mientras éste se adentraba en el sueño a través de la niebla.

"¡Pequeño Cordero!", chilló León, "debes ayudarme."

"¿Cómo puedo ayudarte?", preguntó Pequeño Cordero.

León miró tristemente a Pequeño Cordero y dijo: "Todos los animales vienen a mí con sus problemas. Quieren que yo decida quién está en lo cierto y quién no. Quieren que yo imponga castigo al que ha obrado mal, pero no estoy seguro de estar haciendo lo correcto".

"Cuéntamelo", dijo Pequeño Cordero.

Entonces, León le habló sobre dos bebés zarigüeyas. "Siempre están discutiendo", dijo León. "Su madre me ha pedido que le diga qué hacer".

Pequeño Cordero sonrió a León y dijo: "Nosotros no podemos nunca decidir por nuestra cuenta. Sólo podemos pedir a nuestro Padre que nos ayude a encontrar una respuesta, porque Él, en Su bondad y misericordia, nos enviará la respuesta a cada problema".

Pequeño Cordero y León cerraron sus ojos y se dispusieron a escuchar la respuesta de su Padre. En sus corazones pudieron oír estas palabras:

"Hijos míos, escuchad atentamente: 'La justicia significa ser equitativo. Sólo a través del Amor pueden todos ganar y nadie perder. Dejadme a Mí todos los juicios, ya que Yo amo a todos mis hijos, y amar completamente y a todos por igual es el único juicio que puede existir'".

Entonces, Pequeño Cordero y León fueron al lugar donde los animales esperaban por ellos. Mamá Zarigüeya estaba llorando en silencio. Los bebés zarigüeya esperaban cerca de ella.

León se sentó en su roca y comenzó: "Estáis aquí para pedir mi juicio sobre vuestro problema. Vosotros, bebés zarigüeya, continuáis peleando y discutiendo. Vuestra madre es infeliz y vosotros sois infelices. Vamos a solucionar este problema preguntando a nuestro Padre lo que debemos hacer".

Entonces, todos cerraron los ojos y pidieron ayuda a su Padre. Cada uno de ellos oyó una respuesta en su corazón.

León miró hacia arriba y dijo: "Mi respuesta es dejar todo juicio a nuestro Padre, ya que Su juicio es amar a todos por igual. Todos deben ganar y nadie debe perder. El castigo hace perdedores. El Amor crea ganadores".

Mamá Zarigüeya miró hacia arriba y dijo: "Mi respuesta es amar a mis dos hijos por igual y confiar en el Amor del uno por el otro, ya que, a través de su propio Amor, decidirán lo que deben hacer".

Mientras los bebés zarigüeya se sonreían el uno al otro, el mayor dijo: "Mi respuesta es parar y preguntar a nuestro Padre qué hacer cada vez que empecemos a pelear".

A continuación, el más pequeño dijo: "...Y cuando escuchamos la respuesta de Dios, Él siempre nos muestra Su Amor, y entonces queremos compartir ese Amor con los demás. ¿Quién podría permanecer enfadado cuando está compartiendo Amor?". Los dos bebés zarigüeya se sonrieron mutuamente de nuevo.

León miró amablemente a los zarigüeya y dijo: "Hemos pedido ayuda a nuestro Padre, y Su juicio es amar por igual y confiar en que se comparta ese Amor. Id ahora y jugad. Hoy todos hemos aprendido bien nuestra lección".

Mientras la familia zarigüeya se adentraba en el bosque, Pequeño Cordero y León se sentaron juntos felizmente. En sus corazones podían sentir el Amor y la sabiduría de Dios, el único juicio real.

El Milagro

"Pequeño Cordero", llamó Dios.

"Sí, Padre", contestó Pequeño Cordero.

"Uno de tus hermanos está soñando y necesita tu ayuda. En el sueño ha olvidado la perfección que Yo le di. Duerme, Pequeño Cordero, y sueña. Adéntrate en el sueño y ayuda a tu hermano".

Y en el sueño, Pequeño Cordero abrió sus ojos. Grandes sombras cubrían el suelo del bosque. Pequeño Cordero pudo oír a alguien llorando.

"¡Oh! ¡Oh! Mi pata está rota. Me duele mucho".

Tumbada en el suelo cubierta de musgo había una cierva moteada. Sus ojos estaban cerrados de dolor, y su pata trasera estaba extrañamente torcida.

Pequeño Cordero se dirigió rápidamente hacia la cierva. Corriendo alrededor de ella había un pequeño ratón. "¡Oh, señor! ¡Oh, señor!", decía continuamente Ratón. "La Señorita Cierva es muy grande para que un pequeño ratón como yo la mueva. ¡Oh, señor!, ¿cómo puedo ayudarla?".

Búho, sentado sobre una rama por encima de sus cabezas, gemía: "Nadie puede ayudarla ahora. Es su final. Si ella no puede correr, nunca será capaz de protegerse o encontrar comida para alimentarse. Nadie puede ayudarla ahora".

Y al oír aquello, la cierva lloraba más fuerte, ya que estaba asustada y dolorida.

Pequeño Cordero bajó su vista hacia la cierva y sonrió amablemente. "Yo sé quién puede ayudarte, Señorita Cierva. Si es tu voluntad, escuchas y tienes fe, tu pierna será curada".

La cierva miró hacia arriba con esperanza en sus ojos y dijo: "Escucharé, Pequeño Cordero. Quiero creer".

"Congregaos alrededor, Ratón y Búho", dijo Pequeño Cordero. "Vuestra hermana necesita toda nuestra ayuda. Junto con nuestro Padre curaremos su pierna".

Ratón y Búho fueron despacio hacia ella y se sentaron cerca de la Señorita Cierva. Todos estaban sentados en silencio cuando Pequeño Cordero habló.

"Dios nuestro Padre es Amor. Él sólo puede crear cosas amorosas y Él os creó a vosotros. Dios nuestro Padre es perfecto. Él sólo puede crear cosas perfectas y Él os creó a vosotros. ¿Creéis que nuestro Padre es perfecto y amoroso y crea sólo cosas perfectas y amorosas?", preguntó Pequeño Cordero.

Ratón sintió el beso de Dios en la calidez del sol y dijo: "Sí, creo".

Búho escuchó la canción de Dios en el zumbido de los insectos y dijo: "Sí, creo".

La Señorita Cierva miró a los otros animales y vio a cada uno de ellos resplandeciendo con el Amor de Dios y dijo: "Sí, yo creo".

Estando todos sentados sintiendo el Amor y la perfección de los otros, la bruma del sueño comenzó a aclararse y pudieron ver dónde estaban realmente. Aquí estaba el mundo perfecto de Dios. Nunca lo habían dejado. Y por un Instante Santo, Pequeño Cordero, la Señorita Cierva, Ratón y Búho estuvieron despiertos de nuevo en la paz y la perfección del mundo de su Padre.

Pero un instante no dura, y cuando ellos miraron de nuevo estaban de vuelta en el sueño. Pero algo maravilloso había ocurrido.

"¡Mira! ¡Mira!", exclamó la Señorita Cierva. "Mi pata está curada. Ya no me duele. Puedo incluso caminar con ella". Y mientras los otros animales miraban, la Señorita Cierva se levantó sobre sus patas y comenzó a bailar alrededor alegremente.

"Es un milagro", dijo Ratón.

"¿Cómo es posible?", preguntó Búho.

Pequeño Cordero sonrió. "Ciertamente, a través del Amor de Dios todo es posible. Nos vimos a nosotros mismos amorosos y perfectos, tal y como nuestro Padre nos hizo... y así como Dios nos dio el regalo de un milagro, así podemos recordar Su Amor y nuestra perfección".

La brisa agitó suavemente la lana de Pequeño Cordero.

Al abrir los ojos, Pequeño Cordero vio que estaba despierto en el mundo de su Padre una vez más.

"Has hecho bien hoy, Hijo mío", dijo la Voz de su Padre dentro de su corazón. "Hoy, durante un Instante Santo, tus hermanos despertaron de su sueño y sintieron el Amor, que siempre tengo para ellos, y a través de ese Amor se hizo el regalo de un milagro".

A Través de la Niebla

"¡Pequeño Cordero, Pequeño Cordero! ¡Ayúdame! Estoy solo y asustado. ¡Pequeño Cordero, por favor, ayúdame!".

Pequeño Cordero oyó la llamada de ayuda y se internó en el sueño. Iría y ayudaría a su hermano necesitado.

Mapache estaba acurrucado en el suelo. Su pequeño cuerpo se sacudía con miedo. A su alrededor giraba una niebla oscura y había nubes negras de aspecto enfadado.

Pequeño Cordero apareció al lado de Mapache. "¡Estoy tan solo y asustado!", dijo Mapache a Pequeño Cordero.

"¿De qué estás asustado?", preguntó Pequeño Cordero.

"¿No lo ves? Todo a mi alrededor son nubes oscuras. La niebla es tan oscura que no puedo ver a través de ella. Cuando miro atentamente a la niebla veo cosas", dijo Mapache sacudiéndose más y más según miraba a su alrededor.

"¿Qué cosas piensas que ves en la niebla?", preguntó Pequeño Cordero.

"Veo todas la cosas a las que tengo miedo. Cuando miro a la niebla, me veo a mí mismo herido. Me veo a mí mismo solo y sin nadie que me ame. Estoy tan asustado. ¿Qué puedo hacer...?". Mapache levantó la vista hacia Pequeño Cordero y sus ojos se llenaron de miedo e infelicidad.

El corazón de Pequeño Cordero se abrió hacia su amigo. Sabía exactamente lo que debía hacer para ayudar a Mapache.

"¿Tienes fe en mi Amor por ti?", preguntó Pequeño Cordero a Mapache.

"Sí, la tengo", dijo Mapache.

"¿Quieres dejar atrás estas pesadillas de bruma y adentrarte en la luz?", preguntó Pequeño Cordero.

"Sí, quiero", dijo Mapache lleno de esperanza.

"Entonces, camina conmigo sólo un pequeño trecho. Camina conmigo a través de la niebla del sueño, porque esto es lo que tú ves. Tus pesadillas no son reales. Son sólo reflejos de tus miedos en la niebla que te rodea. De la misma manera en que un espejo reflejaría tu ceñuda cara, así también la niebla de tu alrededor refleja tus pensamientos de miedo. Sígueme y ve cuán irreales son tus miedos". Entonces, Pequeño Cordero comenzó a caminar a través de las nubes oscuras.

Mapache quería creer a Pequeño Cordero porque sabía que él lo amaba. De este modo, hizo acopio de su coraje y siguió a Pequeño Cordero dentro de las nubes oscuras.

Según caminaban uno al lado del otro, la niebla comenzó a apartarse. Todas las pesadillas de miedo que Mapache veía en la niebla comenzaron a desaparecer.

"¡Mira!", chilló Mapache. A través de la niebla Mapache pudo ver la luz brillando. Cuanto más se acercaban a la luz, menos niebla había, hasta que pronto caminaron juntos dentro de la brillante y amorosa luz. Toda la niebla había desaparecido y, con ella, todas las pesadillas de miedo.

Mapache levantó su vista hacia la luz brillante. El cálido Amor de Dios le rodeaba. El miedo se había ido, y sólo la felicidad y la paz permanecían en su corazón.

Mapache miró a Pequeño Cordero y dijo con sorpresa: "Mis pesadillas no eran reales, ¿verdad? Tan pronto como vi la luz y la seguí, la niebla comenzó a desaparecer. Ahora puedo ver dónde estoy realmente. Estoy en el mundo de Dios y he estado aquí todo el tiempo. Yo simplemente no lo veía".

Pequeño Cordero sonrió: "Sí, Mapache. Así como la calidez del sol hace que la niebla de la mañana desaparezca, así también la calidez de Amor de Dios hará desaparecer tus pesadillas de niebla".

Mientras Pequeño Cordero y Mapache permanecían juntos rodeados por la luz de Amor de Dios, pudieron oír la Voz de Dios en ellos y a su alrededor diciendo: "Bienvenido. He estado esperando a que despertases. Ven y permanece en paz en el mundo Real de Amor y felicidad".

La Vida Eterna

"Pequeño Cordero", dijo Dios. "Tu trabajo está casi terminado. Adéntrate en el mundo del sueño de nuevo. Tus hermanos necesitan saber que la vida dura para siempre".

Según entró Pequeño Cordero en el sueño pudo oír a la Señorita Cierva hablando en voz alta: "Pero fue un milagro. Por un Instante Santo, Pequeño Cordero, los otros animales y yo estuvimos en el mundo Real de Dios y mi pata rota se curó".

"No me lo creo", gritó Antílope mientras sus astas se estremecían con enfado, "todo fue un truco. Los milagros no pueden ocurrir realmente y ¡éste es el único mundo que existe!". Y, con esto, Antílope se giró hacia Pequeño Cordero. "Es todo culpa tuya por dar estas ideas peligrosas a los animales".

En su enfado, Antílope bajó sus astas y golpeó a Pequeño Cordero tirándolo al suelo. Al caer, se golpeó la cabeza con una gran piedra y quedó tumbado, inmóvil.

Por un momento, hubo un silencio aterrador. Entonces, la Señorita Cierva comenzó a gritar: "¡Pequeño Cordero está muerto! ¡Pequeño Cordero está muerto!". Y comenzó a gritar con más fuerza.

Todos los demás animales empezaron a congregarse alrededor, algunos llorando, pero todos ellos atemorizados.

A través de la niebla del sueño, Pequeño Cordero observó a sus amigos de pie y llorando alrededor de su cuerpo.

Pequeño Cordero habló a Dios, su Padre, sin palabras: "¿Qué haré ahora, Padre? Todos mis hermanos están tristes y asustados porque he dejado mi cuerpo. Piensan que he muerto y que no viviré más".

Dios habló a Pequeño Cordero: "Regresa al sueño, Pequeño Cordero. Muéstrales que el cuerpo es sólo parte del sueño. Muéstrales que usan el cuerpo para aprender. Muéstrales que yo les he hecho realmente perfectos y que no hay muerte, sólo hermosa vida".

"Hermanos míos", habló Pequeño Cordero a los corazones de sus amigos: "No existe la muerte, ya que aún estoy vivo."

La Señorita Cierva miró a su alrededor y dijo llena de esperanza: "Pero, ¿dónde estás Pequeño Cordero? Puedo oír tu voz en mi corazón, pero no puedo verte. ¡Tu cuerpo está tan inmóvil!".

Como los otros animales también oían a Pequeño Cordero en sus corazones y escuchaban, Pequeño Cordero dijo: "Estoy aquí con vosotros siempre, precisamente de la misma manera en que nuestro Padre siempre está con vosotros. Estoy en el aire que respiráis, el agua que bebéis, las nubes que veis y la hierba sobre la que permanecéis. Estoy en vuestros corazones, ya que aquí es donde está el mundo Real de Dios, y aquí hay vida para siempre".

Mientras los animales miraban, el cuerpo de Pequeño Cordero comenzó a moverse ligeramente. Sus ojos comenzaron a parpadear y su pecho se movió con respiraciones profundas. Antílope exclamó: "¡Está vivo! ¡Pequeño Cordero vive! ¡Ha regresado a la vida!".

Pequeño Cordero se puso de pie despacio y sonrió a todos sus amigos. Al mirar a su alrededor pudo ver a la Señorita Cierva sonriendo con felicidad y Amor. Los ojos de Antílope estaban muy abiertos, llenos de asombro y deleite. Y todos los animales estaban tranquilos y llenos de feliz sorpresa.

"Ciertamente", dijo Antílope, "los milagros sí ocurren, ya que he podido ver ahora que el mundo de Dios está siempre a nuestro alrededor".

"Sí", dijo la Señorita Cierva; "y en el mundo de Dios todos somos perfectos".

Pequeño Cordero sonrió a sus amigos y dijo: "Sí, el mundo de nuestro Padre está lleno de Amor y belleza, y en Su mundo nunca podría haber muerte, sólo hermosa vida que dura para siempre".

Mientras los animales permanecían de pie mirando a Pequeño Cordero, un gran rayo de luz cayó sobre él y pareció resplandecer. En sus corazones todos los animales pudieron oír la Voz de Dios diciendo: "Éste es vuestro hermano en quien me complazco. Hoy estáis en Mi mundo Real juntos. Venid y disfrutad de la belleza y el Amor que yo os doy a todos. Ya que yo amo a todos y cada uno de Mis hijos y les doy el regalo de la vida eterna".

¿ Y Quien Nos Salvara ?

Todos los animales del bosque estaban esperando a Pequeño Cordero. En el centro del círculo había una gran piedra para que Pequeño Cordero se sentase. En la piedra había una corona hecha de margaritas blancas. Los animales estaban callados mientras esperaban que apareciera Pequeño Cordero. Él se introdujo en el sueño y vio a sus hermanos esperándole.

Mamá Petirrojo se acercó y se encontró con Pequeño Cordero. Ella dijo: "Ven, siéntate en la roca en el centro del círculo. Éste será tu trono, y aquí tienes una corona de margaritas para ponerla en tu cabeza".

Pequeño Cordero miró a sus amigos y preguntó: "¿Por qué habéis hecho un trono y una corona para mí?".

Mamá Petirrojo contestó: "Queremos que seas nuestro rey. Queremos que nos dirijas y tomes las decisiones por nosotros, ya que tú eres sabio y amoroso".

Entonces, la Señorita Cierva habló en voz alta: "Tú tienes el poder de realizar milagros".

Y Oso dijo: "Tú hablas con Dios. Tú eres Su Hijo. Por tanto, queremos adorarte".

Pequeño Cordero miró a su alrededor tristemente: "Hermanos míos", dijo, "yo hablo con Dios y cuando escucho Su Palabra soy sabio y amoroso. Pero vosotros no podéis adorarme. Pues, aunque yo soy Hijo de Dios, vosotros también lo sois. Todos somos los Hijos de Dios, y Él ha dado Su Amor, Su poder y Su sabiduría a todos Sus hijos. Yo no puedo tomar vuestras decisiones. Debéis escuchar la Voz de Dios vosotros mismos. Yo soy poderoso y sabio porque escucho la Voz de Dios, y Él me dice qué debo hacer".

"Pero Pequeño Cordero", dijo la Señorita Cierva, "tú haces milagros".

Pequeño Cordero dijo suavemente: "No, Señorita Cierva. Yo no hago milagros. Los milagros son un regalo de Dios porque recordamos Su Amor por nosotros y la perfección que Él nos ha dado".

Entonces, Antílope habló en voz alta: "Tú estabas muerto y volviste a la vida. ¿Es eso algo especial que sólo tú puedes hacer?".

Pequeño Cordero sonrió a Antílope y dijo: "Dios no muere, ya que vive eternamente. Yo soy Hijo de Dios, tal y como vosotros lo sois. Yo vivo eternamente y vosotros también".

"Entonces, ¿quién nos guiará de vuelta a Dios? ¿Quién nos llevará al cielo? ¿Quién nos salvará?", preguntaron todos los animales.

Mientras permanecían sentados tranquilamente esperando la respuesta, la Voz de Dios habló a todos y cada uno de ellos en su corazón: "Hijos míos, todos vosotros sois salvadores del mundo. Sois todos Mis hijos, y unidos, SÓLO unidos, Mi Amor será compartido y completado. Cuando veáis Mi Amor en cada uno de vuestros hermanos, entonces me conoceréis. Cuando deis Mi Amor a cada uno de vuestros hermanos entonces conoceréis el cielo. ¿Quién puede salvaros? Pues, vosotros podéis, ya que junto a vuestros hermanos salvaréis el mundo".

La Señorita Cierva miró a Mamá Petirrojo y a Antílope y dijo: "Vosotros sois mis hermanos y todos nosotros somos hijos de Dios. Donde Sus hijos están, allí está Él. Ahora sé dónde está el cielo. ¡Aquí mismo, ahora mismo!".

...Y los animales se miraron unos a otros con Amor y comprensión. Dios estaba con Sus hijos y ellos estaban en el cielo con Él.

Juntos Al Fin

Dios habló a Pequeño Cordero en su corazón: "Ahora todos tus hermanos y hermanas están preparados para volver a casa. Entra en el último sueño y guía a mis hijos de vuelta a casa". Mientras Pequeño Cordero se adentraba en la niebla del sueño, pudo ver a todos los animales del bosque esperándole.

El sol iluminaba suavemente a cada hermano y hermana haciéndoles resplandecer con el Amor de su Padre. Se sonrieron entre ellos y a Pequeño Cordero, y éste pudo sentir el regalo del Amor de Dios en ellos y a su alrededor.

Pequeño Cordero miró a todos sus hermanos y hermanas y dijo: "Todos habéis aprendido vuestras lecciones aquí en el sueño. El tiempo de dormir y soñar ha terminado. Despertemos y adentrémonos juntos en el mundo de nuestro Padre".

Pequeño Cordero se giró hacia Ardilla Gris, Oso y Gran Ganso: "¿Qué lección aprendisteis para poder despertar en el mundo Real?".

Los tres animales sonrieron y contestaron juntos: "Sólo debemos pedir las respuestas a nuestros problemas y escuchar la Voz amorosa de nuestro Padre, ya que en el Amor de nuestro Padre está la respuesta a todas nuestras preguntas".

Pequeño Cordero sonrió y dijo: "Venid conmigo al mundo de nuestro Padre".

A continuación, Pequeño Cordero miró a las dos ardillas y preguntó: "¿Qué lección aprendisteis para despertar en el mundo Real?".

Y las ardillas contestaron: "Nosotras nos perdonamos mutuamente. El enfado viene del miedo, y el miedo desaparece cuando se comparte el Amor".

Pequeño Cordero sonrió y dijo: "Adentraos conmigo en el mundo de nuestro Padre".

Castor se levantó a continuación, a medida que un claro y brillante rayo de luz descendía sobre su cabeza y dijo: "Mi lección fue elegir la felicidad. Dios me da solamente Amor y bondad. Dependía de mí decidir si quería ver ese Amor y esa bondad".

"Entonces entra conmigo en el mundo de nuestro Padre", dijo Pequeño Cordero.

La Señorita Cierva, seguida de Ratón y de Búho, avanzó y dijo: "Juntos dejamos este sueño por un Instante Santo y vimos el mundo Real de Dios. Mediante el regalo de Amor de Dios me fue dado un milagro y mi pata rota fue curada. Es para nosotros el momento de regresar al mundo de nuestro Padre para siempre".

Pequeño Cordero sonrió y dijo: "Entonces, venid conmigo".

Al mirar Pequeño Cordero a su alrededor, a los otros animales, los dos cisnes hablaron en voz alta: "Nuestra lección es compartir el Amor de Dios juntos". Se sonrieron el uno al otro amorosamente.

Ardilla Gris, Mamá Petirrojo y Rata dijeron todos juntos: "La felicidad está en tu interior. Cuando sientes el regalo de Amor de Dios te sientes feliz y deseas compartirlo con todo el mundo".

Pequeño Cordero sonrió y dijo: "Habéis aprendido bien vuestras lecciones. Venid conmigo al mundo Real de nuestro Padre".

León habló a continuación: "La justicia significa ser completamente equitativo, y sólo el Amor puede hacer que todos ganen y nadie pierda". León y todos los animales sintieron el juicio de Dios en sus corazones. Eran todos hermanos y hermanas y podían sentir el Amor de su Padre por igual.

Antílope se acercó tranquilamente y miró a su alrededor despacio: "Sí, regresemos todos a nuestro Hogar, nuestro Padre, ya que en el sueño vemos pesadillas llenas de muerte. Vemos enfado y miedo en nuestros hermanos y sentimos enfado y miedo en nuestros corazones. Pero en el mundo Real de Dios sólo hay Amor, paz, perdón, perfección y vida hermosa para siempre".

Mapache apareció a través de la niebla, adentrándose en el sueño y dijo: "Hola amigos. He regresado una vez más al sueño para ayudar a Pequeño Cordero a llevaros a casa. Hace algún tiempo, él me ayudó a atravesar la niebla y aprendí mi lección: 'Todas las cosas amenazadoras y que yo creía ver en el sueño eran sólo reflejos de mis propios miedos'".

Pequeño Cordero sonrió a todos sus amigos y dijo: "La hora ha llegado. Recorramos un pequeño camino juntos". Y así lo hicieron. A través de la niebla, caminaron hacia la luz brillante del Amor de su Padre. A medida que avanzaban, la niebla comenzó a desaparecer y la luz brillante y amorosa les rodeó. En sus corazones, todos podían oír la Voz de su Padre: "Bienvenidos a casa. El tiempo del sueño y las pesadillas ha terminado. Ahora es el momento de despertar y ver Mi mundo Real, ya que Yo lo he creado con Amor como el más preciado regalo para Mis hijos. Venid y disfrutad de lo que siempre ha sido vuestro".

...Y los animales entraron en el mundo de su Padre, llenos de felicidad, Amor y perfección.

Libro de Ejercicios

"Traed los niños a mí para en su Inocencia el Amor nazca."

Introducción

Estas meditaciones son enviadas a cada uno de vosotros para que podáis traer la verdad de nuevo a las pequeñas almas con quienes estáis trabajando. Ya seas padre o profesor, tu papel es el Amor y el perdón. A medida que meditéis sobre vuestra función, experimentaréis la conciencia de Dios a través de cada persona. Cada meditación se debería practicar al final de la lección, o en casa por la mañana y por la noche. Éste debería ser un momento de tranquilidad, calidez y ternura, un momento de máxima profundidad juntos; y juntos llegaréis a Dios.

Cada lección se completará con un periodo de quietud, lo que permitirá a los estudiantes y al profesor fundirse juntos en el silencio del Amor de Dios. Éste será el tiempo de meditación para los niños. Los niños, con frecuencia, desarrollan talentos y habilidades al adaptarse a la meditación, pero la mayoría no será capaz de sentarse silenciosamente durante mucho rato. Aquí está el secreto de la meditación de los niños: breve, comprensible y amorosa. El mensaje será alto y claro para cada pequeña alma que escucha con su corazón. No te extrañes si las reacciones de los niños no son las que esperas. El cuerpo de cada niño reacciona de forma diferente ante un estímulo, incluido el de tipo espiritual. Trae paciencia, Amor y perdón contigo a la meditación. Permite a cada niño expresarse individualmente, sin hacer juicios.

Tu meditación de grupo debería tener lugar al final de la lección. Éste es un momento de tranquilidad para que lo pasen contigo. Ellos no necesitan cerrar los ojos, aunque puede ayudar. Aun así, el mensaje del Amor hará su recorrido a través de las capas del ego hasta el corazón de cada pequeña alma.

Lee la meditación lenta y claramente. Luego, repetid las frases clave juntos. Pide a los niños que recuerden esta idea toda la semana o hasta la próxima lección. Ahora, tus tareas del día han terminado. Envía a tus pequeños a casa. Has aprendido tu lección al tiempo que los pequeños aprendieron las suyas.

Lección 1

Dios es Amor
Dios sólo puede crear cosas amorosas
y Dios te creó a ti.

Piensa por un momento sobre quién eres tú y de dónde procedes. Mira a tu padre y luego mírate a ti mismo. ¿Tiene tu padre manos y pies? Tú también. ¿Tiene tu padre brazos y piernas? Tú también. ¿Puede tu padre sonreír y reír? Tú también. ¿Eres como tu padre? Por supuesto que sí.

Ahora piensa en Dios, el Padre de todos y de todo. Dios nuestro Padre está lleno de Amor. Él es Amor. Tú no puedes ver el Amor. Sólo puedes SENTIRLO. ¿Eres como tu Padre? Sí que lo eres. Siente el Amor de tu Padre. Porque eres en verdad el hijo de tu Padre, y al igual que Él está lleno de Amor, tú también lo estás.

(Ahora leed todos en voz alta)

Dios es Amor
Dios sólo puede crear cosas amorosas
y Dios me creó a mí.

Lección 2

Dios sólo da bondad y Amor.
Y Dios te lo da todo.

¿Cómo muestras tú el Amor? Muestras el Amor haciendo cosas amorosas. ¿Cómo Dios tu Padre, quien te ama, te muestra Su Amor? Él te da bondad, felicidad, paz y júbilo.

(Ahora leed todos en voz alta)

Dios sólo da bondad y Amor.
Y Dios me lo da todo.

Lección 3

Dentro de mi cabeza Dios me habla.
Dentro de mi corazón Dios está.

¿Dónde está Dios nuestro Padre? No mires muy lejos, porque Él está dentro de ti. Él es esa luz brillante de Amor que te hace ser quien eres. Él es tu centro. Ahora escucha en silencio su Voz que te quiere ayudar. Él está siempre dentro de ti y te hablará si escuchas con el corazón. ¿No es agradable saber que no estás nunca solo?

(Ahora leed todos en voz alta)

Dentro de mi cabeza Dios me habla.
Dentro de mi corazón Dios está.

Lección 4

Feliz o triste,
Amoroso o atemorizado.
¿Quién decide? Tú decides.

Mira a tu alrededor. ¿Es el mundo brillante y hermoso? ¿O es oscuro y feo? ¿Ves amigos o enemigos? ¿Te sientes feliz y en paz o te sientes solo y asustado? La habitación que ves es sólo una habitación. Tú decides si es fea o bonita. Las personas que ves cada día son todos tus hermanos. Tú decides si ellos son tus amigos o tus enemigos.

Si te sientes solo y asustado es porque así es como has elegido estar. Ahora decidamos estar felices y en paz. Tú eres el Hijo de Dios. Tú puedes ser lo que quieras ser.

(Ahora leed todos en voz alta)

Feliz o triste,
Amoroso o atemorizado.
¿Quién decide? Yo decido.

Lección 5

Feliz o triste
Amoroso o asustado.
¿Quién te ayuda a decidir estar contento?
Dios te ayuda.

Si nosotros somos quienes decidimos estar felices o estar asustados, entonces ¿cómo es posible que haya alguien asustado o infeliz? Podríamos simplemente decidir estar felices. Pero no podemos hacerlo solos. Somos parte de Dios nuestro Padre, Quien está en nosotros, y debemos pedirle que nos ayude a decidir estar felices. Juntos con Dios podemos hacer cualquier cosa; podemos ser cualquier cosa. Cuando estamos juntos con Dios estamos siempre felices. La única decisión que deberíamos tomar es recordar que Dios está siempre con nosotros y entonces estaremos siempre felices.

(Ahora leed todos en voz alta)

Feliz o triste,
Amoroso o asustado.
¿Quién me ayuda a decidir estar contento?
Dios me ayuda.

Lección 6

¿Qué hace que una sombra
sea amenazadora o amistosa?
Tu mente lo hace.

Tu mente te dice qué pensar. Tu mente te dice si te gusta lo que ves o no te gusta lo que ves. Tus ojos ven sombras a tu alrededor. Tu mente decide si son amenazadoras o amistosas, puesto que tú no puedes tocar una sombra y una sombra no te puede tocar. Las sombras no son reales. Es sólo lo que tú decides pensar de ellas lo que las hace parecer reales.

Cuando algo o alguien te asusta, recuerda: "Tú sólo estás viendo sombras". Busca la luz del Amor de Dios y ésta alejará todas las sombras amenazadoras que no son reales.

(Ahora leed todos en voz alta)

¿Qué hace que una sombra
sea amenazadora o amistosa?
Mi mente lo hace.

Lección 7

¿Qué hace que tu mejor amigo
sea un amigo cuando jugáis
pero un enemigo cuando peleáis?
Tu mente lo hace.

Todos somos hermanos. Tenemos el mismo Padre. Él es amoroso y comprensivo; por lo tanto, nosotros somos amorosos y comprensivos. Tu hermano y tú sois lo mismo. Pero tú puedes decidir verle de forma diferente. Puedes decidir que no te gusta. Puedes decidir pelear con él. O puedes decidir amarle, entenderle y ser felices juntos.

¿Por qué querrías pelear y ser infeliz? Tu hermano es exactamente igual que tú. Él es amoroso y comprensivo, y así eres tú también.

(Ahora leed todos en voz alta)

¿Qué hace que mi mejor amigo
sea un amigo cuando jugamos
pero un enemigo cuando peleamos?
Mi mente lo hace.

Lección 8

Sé un perfecto espejo; refleja el Amor de Dios.

Brilla en todo tu esplendor. Elimina todo los pensamientos de odio e ira. Saca brillo al espejo de tu corazón. Porque, al igual que un espejo, tú reflejarás lo que hay en tu corazón. Elimina la suciedad y la basura y refleja en todo su esplendor el Amor de Dios. Su Amor es como una luz que brilla intensamente. Déjala brillar en tu corazón y refleja Amor, aumentando su brillo con cada pensamiento y acto amorosos.

(Ahora leed todos en voz alta)

Yo soy un perfecto espejo; me permito reflejar el Amor de Dios.

Lección 9

La paz y el Amor traen felicidad
y alegría a toda tu vida.
La paz y el Amor traen felicidad
porque Dios vive en ti.

Siempre que estés perdido y con miedo, siempre que las cosas no vayan como tú quieras, recuerda esta pequeña oración. Dios tu Padre está siempre ahí, y donde Él está, encontrarás la paz, la alegría y la felicidad.

(Ahora leed todos en voz alta)

La paz y el Amor traen felicidad
y alegría a toda mi vida.
La paz y el Amor traen felicidad
porque Dios vive en mí.

Lección 10

¿Dónde está Dios?
¿Dónde no está Él?
No necesitas buscar lejos
pues Dios está aquí, ahí y en todas partes.

Escucha calladamente y oirás a tu Padre hablarte. Mira con atención, con ojos amorosos y verás dónde vive tu Padre. Él no está lejos, pues nunca dejaría a Sus Hijos solos. Está donde tú siempre puedes encontrarle. Está justo aquí, ¡ahora mismo!

(Ahora leed todos en voz alta)

¿Dónde está Dios?
¿Dónde no está El?
No necesito buscar lejos
pues Dios está aquí, allí y en todas partes.

Lección 11

Cuando Dios habla, el mundo escucha;
su llamada de Amor nos llena de vida a todos.

Ábrete a escuchar la voz de tu Padre. Te hablará a través de la canción del gorrión, a través de la brisa cálida del verano, a través de la risa feliz de los niños. Su voz te habla de Amor y vida. Pues sin Amor no hay vida. Ábrete a escuchar la Voz de tu Padre; está dentro de tu corazón, y ahí está el Amor.

(Ahora leed todos en voz alta)

Cuando Dios habla, el mundo escucha;
su llamada de Amor nos llena de vida a todos.

Lección 12

Dentro de nuestros corazones,
Dios espera pacientemente.
Dentro del corazón de Dios,
nosotros vivimos y amamos.

Dios conoce a sus niños. Dios comprende a Sus Hijos. Dios está siempre dentro de ti esperando pacientemente a que escuches Su Voz amorosa. ¿Dejaría un padre amoroso a su niño solo y asustado? Siente a Dios dentro de ti y sabrás que Él está en ti y tú estás en Él.

(Ahora leed todos en voz alta)

Dentro de nuestros corazones,
Dios espera pacientemente.
Dentro del corazón de Dios,
nosotros vivimos y amamos.

Lección 13

El viento, Su amable caricia.
El sol, Su tierno beso.
La lluvia, Sus lágrimas de alegría, limpiando y refrescando.
Los pájaros, insectos y animales, Cantando sus canciones de vida.
Y todo esto, Su regalo a Sus niños bien amados.

Gracias, Padre, por el Amor que me das a mí, Tu niño.

(Ahora leed todos en voz alta)

El viento, Su amable caricia.
El sol, Su tierno beso.
La lluvia, Sus lágrimas de alegría, limpiando y refrescando.
Los pájaros, insectos y animales, Cantando sus canciones de vida.
Y todo esto, Su regalo para mí, Su niño bien amado.

Lección 14

Habla sólo de Amor
y sólo la voz de Dios será oída.

Habla al mundo acerca del Amor de Dios y te convertirás en una herramienta para el trabajo de Dios. Oye Su Voz diciéndote qué hacer y luego permite que Sus palabras sean tuyas cuando tú hables. Él sabe lo que es bueno y correcto. Él sabe lo que es amoroso. Escúchale y pronuncia sólo las palabras que oigas en tu corazón. Mira qué fácil es. Y ve cuán feliz te hace.

(Ahora leed todos en voz alta)

Yo sólo hablaré de Amor
y sólo la Voz de Dios será escuchada.

Lección 15

Sólo siente la paz de Dios
y el cielo te envolverá.

Dios está siempre aquí para guiarte y protegerte. Él te mantendrá a salvo y feliz. Todo lo que necesitas hacer es escuchar Su amorosa Voz y sentir su amorosa presencia dentro de ti y a tu alrededor. ¿Dónde está el cielo sino en vuestros corazones? No necesitas mirar lejos. Pues donde Dios está, también está el cielo.

(Ahora leed todos en voz alta)

Sólo siento la paz de Dios
y el cielo me envuelve.

Lección 16

Yo soy uno.
Tú también.
Fíjate bien: los tres, Dios el Padre, tú y yo.
Juntos formamos la trinidad del Amor.

Fíjate bien: los tres — Dios el Padre, tú y yo. Esto es lo que es el Amor. Tú eres parte de Dios; tú eres Su hijo. Tu hermano es parte de Dios; él es el hijo de Dios también. Si has de amar a Dios, debes amar todo lo que es parte de Él. Por lo tanto, debemos amar a nuestros hermanos. Dios ama cada cosa que es Suya. Y nosotros somos Sus niños a quienes Él ama. Fíjate bien, los tres, Dios el Padre tú y yo. Juntos formamos la trinidad del Amor. Juntos somos uno.

(Ahora leed todos en voz alta)

Yo soy uno.
Tú también.
Fíjate bien: los tres, Dios el Padre tú y yo.
Juntos formamos la trinidad del Amor.

Lección 17

Haz de cada día el mejor,
haz que cada minuto sea de paz y de descanso,
haz de cada segundo un momento con Dios.
Esto es el camino a la alegría; esto es un corazón feliz.

Hoy tienes dos elecciones. Puedes recordar que Dios está contigo ahora o puedes olvidar que Él está aquí. Si eliges olvidar que está contigo, te sentirás perdido, solo y asustado. Pero si recuerdas que Él nunca está lejos de ti, amándote y guiándote y protegiéndote siempre, entonces estarás feliz y a salvo.

(Ahora leed todos en voz alta)

Haz de cada día el mejor,
haz que cada minuto sea de paz y descanso,
haz de cada segundo un momento con Dios.
Esto es el camino a la alegría; esto es un corazón feliz.

Lección 18

Cada uno de nosotros es como el otro...
Parte de un todo; cada parte, un hermano.

¿Dónde terminas tú y empiezan tus hermanos? ¿Dónde termina Dios y dónde empieza? Puedes tener un aspecto diferente. Puede que parezcas estar separado de tus hermanos, pero tú no eres sólo tu cuerpo. Tú eres mucho, mucho más. Tú eres espíritu. El espíritu no se puede ver ni tocar, sólo puede ser sentido con el corazón. Ahí es donde está Dios. Esto es Dios. Él es espíritu, y tú, también. Tú eres uno junto con Dios y tus hermanos. Sois parte del todo, y todos juntos completáis el Amor de Dios.

(Ahora leed todos en voz alta)

Cada uno de nosotros es como el otro...
Parte de un todo; cada parte, un hermano.

Lección 19

Siempre que te sientas solo
simplemente mira y ve Quién está contigo.
Con cada respiración que tomes,
siente la presencia de Dios. Él está en ti.

Él es quien te ayuda. Es tu amigo. Él es quien te ayuda en cualquier momento que se lo pidas. Él te ama y está siempre contigo. Respira profundamente y siente Su Amor llenándote. Tú eres Su Hijo a quien Él ama.

(Ahora leed todos en voz alta)

Siempre que me siento solo
simplemente miro y veo Quién está conmigo.
Con cada respiración que tomo,
siento la presencia de Dios. Él está en mí.

Lección 20

Una sonrisa, una mirada, una palabra de ayuda...
Oraciones de Amor de hermano a hermano.

¿Cuál es la forma más agradable de decir te quiero? Puede ser simplemente mostrar una cara sonriente a alguien que está triste. Puede ser simplemente una mirada de Amor cuando alguien siente que es malo. Pueden ser simplemente una o dos palabras para ayudar a alguien que se siente triste. No importa la forma que tenga el Amor siempre que sea Amor lo que estás dando.

(Ahora leed todos en voz alta)

Una sonrisa, una mirada, una palabra de ayuda...
Oraciones de Amor que doy a mis hermanos.

Siempre que alguien parezca decir
"No te quiero, márchate",
mira dentro de él en lo más profundo,
pues el Amor está ahí,
muy escondido bajo su miedo.
Miedo de que tú tampoco le ames.
Pero tú realmente le quieres, y él te quiere.
Por lo tanto, siempre que alguien parezca decir
"No te quiero, márchate",
mira dentro, en lo más profundo,
pues el Amor está aquí,
resplandeciendo con fuerza, siempre a tu lado.

No te dejes engañar por la cara y las palabras de enfado de alguien. Escucha muy atentamente, pues lo que realmente están diciendo es que están asustados y no se sienten amados. Su enfado es una petición de ayuda y Amor. Ayudemos a todos nuestros hermanos. Todo lo que necesitamos hacer es amarles. ¿Quién podría permanecer enfadado cuando le envuelve el Amor?

(Ahora leed todos en voz alta)

Siempre que alguien parezca decir
"No te quiero, márchate",
mira dentro de él en lo más profundo,
pues el Amor está ahí,
muy escondido bajo su miedo.
Miedo de que tú tampoco le ames.
Pero tú realmente le quieres, y él te quiere.
Por lo tanto, siempre que alguien parezca decir
"No te quiero, márchate",
mira dentro en lo más profundo, pues el Amor está aquí,
resplandeciendo con fuerza, siempre a tu lado.

Lección 22

Para conocer tu corazón,
mira en los ojos de tu hermano.

Tu hermano es un espejo de ti mismo. ¿Qué ves en él? ¿Ves rabia, miedo, tristeza? ¿O ves felicidad, paz, alegría? Si no te gusta lo que ves en tu hermano, entonces mira dentro de ti y cámbialo ahí. Tu hermano es simplemente un espejo de ti mismo. Siéntete feliz y amoroso y verás felicidad y Amor reflejados en tu hermano.

(Ahora leed todos en voz alta)

Para conocer mi corazón,
debo mirar en los ojos de mi hermano.

Lección 23

Si mantienes el pensamiento de dolor y sufrimiento,
estarás atrapado y ahí permanecerás.
Pero si mantienes el pensamiento de alegría y salud
conocerás la paz de Dios, Su Amor, Su riqueza.

Tú eres un Hijo de Dios. Puedes ser lo que desees ser. Elige felicidad y serás feliz. Elige miedo y rabia y serás infeliz. Elige enfermedad y dolor y tendrás eso también. Todo lo que necesitas hacer es PENSAR en ello, y será tuyo. ¿Qué deseas?: ¿Felicidad o infelicidad, Amor o miedo, salud o enfermedad? Dios quiere que seas feliz, amoroso y saludable. Pensemos Sus pensamientos.

(Ahora leed todos en voz alta)

Si yo mantengo el pensamiento de dolor y sufrimiento,
estaré atrapado y ahí permaneceré.
Pero ahora mantengo el pensamiento de alegría y salud
y conozco la paz de Dios, Su Amor, Su riqueza.

Lección 24

Todas nuestras mentes son una.
Estamos conectados.
Estamos conectados en el pensamiento.
Estamos conectados en el Amor.
Pues el Amor es pensamiento expresado a todos.

Todos somos hijos de Dios. Todos estamos conectados por el Amor. Y el Amor es sólo un pensamiento. Pensamos con nuestras mentes. Y nuestras mentes son una. Todo lo que necesitamos hacer es pensar en el Amor y seremos uno con todos nuestros hermanos y todos con Dios al instante. ¿No es el Amor maravilloso?

(Ahora leed todos en voz alta)

Todas nuestras mentes son una.
Estamos conectados.
Estamos conectados en el pensamiento.
Estamos conectados en el Amor.
Pues el Amor es pensamiento expresado a todos.

Lección 25

Abre bien tus ojos y tu corazón,
como los pétalos de una flor.
Abre bien tus ojos y tu corazón
para sentir el Amor y el poder de Dios.

¿Has mirado últimamente a tu alrededor con atención? ¿Has escuchado detenidamente? ¿Qué ves y oyes? Si realmente miras y escuchas, oirás La Voz de Dios llamándote en el murmullo de las hojas al viento o el estruendo de un tren de mercancías, o la risa feliz de tus amigos y familiares. Él está siempre ahí. Sólo mira atentamente y escucha. Puedes oírle ahora. Te está diciendo: "Te amo".

(Ahora leed todos en voz alta)

Abro bien mis ojos y mi corazón,
como los pétalos de una flor.
Abro bien mis ojos y mi corazón
y siento el Amor y el poder de Dios.

Lección 26

Tú estás en la Mente de Dios;
por lo tanto, piensa Sus pensamientos.

Si Dios es Amor, ¿entonces qué clase de pensamientos podría tener Dios? Por supuesto, pensamientos amorosos. Si eres el Hijo de Dios, entonces tú eres también. ¿Qué clase de pensamientos tendrías tú? Por supuesto, pensamientos amorosos. Escucha la Voz de tu Padre y piensa Sus pensamientos con Él, pues son tus pensamientos también. Te pertenecen. Piensa Amor, pues tú eres Amor.

(Ahora leed todos en voz alta)

Estoy en la mente de Dios;
por lo tanto, pienso Sus pensamientos.

Lección 27

¿Dónde está el mundo de Dios?
Aquí mismo, ahora mismo.
¿Puedes ver el mundo de Dios?
Sí, con ojos amorosos; ésa es la forma de verlo.

El cielo no está a mucha distancia. El cielo está aquí mismo. Cada vez que te sientes lleno de Amor y felicidad, estás recordando tu verdadero hogar. Cada vez que compartes Amor con tus hermanos, estás dando un pedazo de cielo a alguien, y el cielo crece cuando haces esto. ¿Dónde está el cielo? Aquí mismo, ahora mismo.

(Ahora leed todos en voz alta)

¿Dónde está el mundo de Dios?
Aquí mismo, ahora mismo.
¿Puedo ver el mundo de Dios?
Sí, con ojos amorosos; ésa es la forma de verlo.

Lección 28

Manténte siempre alerta para escuchar los pensamientos de Dios.
Son pensamientos de Amor.
Son pensamientos que sanan.
Son pensamientos de unicidad
para comprender y sentir la unicidad.

Escucha atentamente los pensamientos que piensas. Siempre sabrás cuándo estás pensando los Pensamientos de Dios con Él. Sus pensamientos te hacen feliz. Sus pensamientos te hacen bien. Sus pensamientos están llenos de Amor y alegría. Sus pensamientos son tuyos. Lo que necesitas hacer es pensarlos.

(Ahora leed todos en voz alta)

Manténte siempre alerta para escuchar los pensamientos de Dios.
Son pensamientos de Amor.
Son pensamientos que sanan.
Son pensamientos de unicidad
para comprender y sentir la unicidad.

Lección 29

¿Dolor y muerte o
alegría y vida?
La elección es tuya.

¿Quién decide cómo será tu cuerpo? ¿Es fuerte? ¿Es saludable? ¿Es débil? ¿Está enfermo? ¿Cómo crearía Dios tu cuerpo? ¿Te crearía enfermo? Nunca. ¿Te crearía débil? Nunca. ¿Te crearía fuerte y saludable? ¡Por supuesto! Él te ama. Él te da todo. Pero te corresponde a ti aceptar Sus regalos. ¿Cuál es tu elección?

(Ahora leed todos en voz alta)

¿Dolor y muerte o
alegría y vida?
La elección es mía.

Lección 30

El regalo que Dios te da es la vida.

La vida es algo más que inspirar y espirar. La vida es ser feliz. La vida es sentir paz y alegría. La vida es saber que Dios está siempre contigo. La vida nunca termina. La vida es eterna. Y es siempre tuya.

(Ahora leed todos en voz alta)

El regalo que Dios me da es la vida.

Lección 31

Coloca tus manos en las de Dios y Él te guiará a casa.

Las manos amorosas de tu Padre están siempre ahí para ayudarte. En tu corazón escucharás Su Voz, guiándote y mostrándote el camino. Y a medida que escuches sentirás Sus manos cogiendo las tuyas y guiándote a un lugar seguro. El hogar de Dios es tu hogar. El hogar de Dios es el cielo, y tú nunca lo has abandonado.

(Ahora leed todos en voz alta)

Coloco mis manos en las de Dios
y Él me guiará a casa.

Lección 32

Sánate a ti mismo pidiéndole ayuda a Dios.

Si Dios no te hace enfermar, entonces ¿quién lo hace? Tú lo haces. Tú eliges la enfermedad o el dolor o la infelicidad. ¿Cómo puedes llegar a ser saludable y feliz? Simplemente cambiando tu mente. ¿Puedes hacerlo solo? No, tú no puedes. Ése es el motivo por el que Dios siempre está ahí para ayudarte. Todo lo que tienes que hacer es pedir.

(Ahora leed todos en voz alta)

Me sano a mí mismo pidiéndole ayuda a Dios.

Lección 33

Cambia tu mente y cambia el mundo. Sánate a ti mismo, y el mundo sanará contigo.

Tú eres una parte de Dios, y Dios es una parte de todo y todos. Tú estás en Dios, y Dios está en todo y todos. Tú eres un pensamiento de Dios, y todas las cosas y todos nosotros somos pensamientos de Dios. Nunca estás solo y lo que piensas y haces afecta a todo, pues tú eres una parte de Dios.

(Ahora leed todos en voz alta)

Cambio mi mente y cambio el mundo.
Me sano a mí mismo, y el mundo sanará conmigo.

Lección 34

Tu hermano comparte sus pensamientos contigo.
Tus pensamientos son tuyos; falsos o verdaderos.
Los pensamientos verdaderos traen Amor;
los pensamientos falsos traen dolor.
¿Cuáles pensarías tú?
¿Cuáles seguirías?
¿Cuáles regalarías a tu hermano?
¿Cuáles querrías que tu hermano te regalara?
Tu hermano comparte sus pensamientos contigo.
Tus pensamientos son suyos; falsos o verdaderos.
Los pensamientos verdaderos traen Amor;
los pensamientos falsos traen dolor.

(Ahora leed todos en voz alta)

Doy el regalo de Amor a mi hermano.

Lección 35

Compartir, ayudar, amar, sentir.
Pensamientos de Dios, pensamientos de sanación.

Los pensamientos de Dios están siempre en tu mente. Pero algunas veces los olvidamos. Todo lo que debemos hacer es pensar en cosas amorosas que queremos realizar por nuestros hermanos. Todo en lo que necesitamos pensar es en la felicidad, la alegría, el compartir y la ayuda. Éstos son los Pensamientos de Dios, y son nuestros pensamientos también. Ayúdate a ti mismo y ayuda a tu hermano hoy. ¡Qué maravilloso y qué simple es!

(Ahora leed todos en voz alta)

Al compartir, ayudar, amar, sentir,
pienso los Pensamientos de Dios;
pienso en la sanación.

Lección 36

Tómate tiempo para amar a tu hermano.

Mira todas las cosas que tu mente piensa a lo largo del día. Piensa en todos los pensamientos que tienes. ¿Cuántos de tus pensamientos son sobre tus hermanos? ¿Cuántos de tus pensamientos sobre tus hermanos son pensamientos amorosos? Pasemos más tiempo pensando pensamientos amorosos sobre nuestros hermanos.

(Ahora leed todos en voz alta)

Me tomaré tiempo para amar a mi hermano.

Lección 37

¿Dónde encontrarás a tu Padre? Tras la mirada de tu hermano encontrarás la de Dios.

Dios nuestro Padre no está lejos. Dios vive en ti, vive en mí y vive dentro de tu hermano. Todo lo que necesitas hacer para encontrar a tu Padre y Su Amor, es mirar bien de cerca a tu hermano. Ahí está el Amor y ahí está la felicidad. Mira profundamente en los ojos de tu hermano y descubre el hogar de Dios, el tuyo y el mío.

(Ahora leed todos en voz alta)

¿Dónde encontraré a mi Padre?
Tras la mirada de mi hermano encontraré la de Dios.

Lección 38

Para encontrar a tu Padre mira en el interior de tu hermano

No ignores el regalo de Amor de tu hermano. Es el regalo de Amor que tu Padre te da a través de tu hermano. Ahí, en tu hermano, está el hogar que has estado buscando. Ahí, en el Amor de tu hermano, encontrarás el Amor que estás buscando. Ahí está Dios, ahí está el cielo, ahí está la alegría.

(Ahora leed todos en voz alta)

Para encontrar a mi Padre
debo mirar en el interior de mi hermano.

Lección 39

La felicidad es compartida por todos.

Mira cuán contagiosa es una sonrisa. Mira cuán contagiosa es la risa. Ríe abiertamente y sonríe, y el mundo querrá unirse a ti. Ahora piensa en los pensamientos que te hacen reír. También son contagiosos. Ofrece al mundo algunas risas y sonrisas. Te sentirás bien y el mundo se sentirá bien contigo.

(Ahora leed todos en voz alta)

Mi felicidad es compartida por todos.

Lección 40

Abre tus ojos y mira a tu hermano...
brillando con fuerza, brillando con claridad;
un espejo de tu Amor,
un reflejo de tu Padre.

Tu hermano es el espejo de tu Amor. Deja que tu Amor brille con fuerza para que pueda reflejarse en tu hermano y bendecirte a ti con felicidad. Ve a tu hermano amado y amoroso y serás amado y amoroso también.

(Ahora leed todos en voz alta)

Abro mis ojos y veo a mi hermano...
brillando con fuerza, brillando con claridad;
un espejo de mi Amor,
un reflejo de mi Padre.

Lección 41

¿Quién te habla cuando estás solo?
¿Quién te guía y dirige hacia tu hogar?
Dios lo hace.

Ahora sabes quién es el que más te ama. Ahora sabes dónde encontrar Su Amor. Ahora sabes cómo oír la Voz amorosa de tu Padre. Escucha silenciosamente Su Voz, pues te mostrará el camino hacia tu hogar. Te mostrará la felicidad y la alegría. Es la Voz del Amor.

(Ahora leed todos en voz alta)

¿Quién me habla cuando estoy solo?
¿Quién me guía y me dirige hacia mi hogar?
Dios lo hace.

Lección 42

Recuerda quién y qué eres; recuerda que eres el mismísimo Hijo de Dios.

Dios es espíritu. Y tú también. Dios es Amor. Y tú también. Dios da felicidad y alegría, y esto es lo que tú recibes. Dios crea el cielo, y ése es tu hogar. Dios es tu Padre, y tú eres Su Hijo. ¡Qué familia tan maravillosa tenemos!

(Ahora leed todos en voz alta)

Yo recuerdo quién soy y lo que soy;
recuerdo que soy el mismísimo Hijo de Dios,
y soy feliz.

Lección 43

El Amor brota a través de tu mente. El mismísimo Amor de Dios es tuyo, es mío.

Siente el enorme poder del Amor. El Amor te trae todo lo que necesitas. Te trae Amor, felicidad y paz. Te conecta con todos tus hermanos. Te conecta con tu Padre. El Amor es como el poderoso lazo que nos une a todos. Siente el Amor de Dios y aprende que es tuyo para siempre.

(Ahora leed todos en voz alta)

El Amor brota a través de mi mente.
El mismísimo Amor de Dios es tuyo, es mío.

Lección 44

Abre completamente tu corazón y aprende: Dios está aquí, y el cielo es ahora

Miramos a todas partes para encontrar las cosas que nos harán felices. Algunas veces creemos que será un juguete, pero pronto nos cansamos de él. Algunas veces creemos que es visitar un lugar, pero la diversión que tenemos sólo nos dura un momento.

No tienes que mirar lejos para encontrar la felicidad. La felicidad es Dios, y Dios está siempre contigo. La felicidad es el cielo, y el hogar del cielo está en el Amor de Dios. No mires lejos, pues Dios está aquí y el cielo es ahora.

(Ahora leed todos en voz alta)

Abro completamente mi corazón y aprendo:
Dios está aquí, y el cielo es ahora.

Lección 45

Fe y confianza, esperanza y Amor; oraciones y regalos a Dios.

Dios nos da todo. Él nos da el más preciado regalo de todos: Su Amor. Y Su Amor nos hará felices y pacíficos. ¿Qué nos pide Dios a cambio? El único regalo que quiere nuestro Padre es que tengamos fe y confianza en Su Amor por nosotros. ¡Qué sencillo es! Todo lo que necesitamos hacer es amar a los demás y recibiremos de vuelta el regalo de Amor de Dios.

(Ahora leed todos en voz alta)

Fe y confianza, esperanza y Amor;
oraciones y regalos a Dios.

Lección 46

Deposita tu fe en Dios, tu Padre.
Él te guía de vuelta a tu hogar;
a ti y a tu hermano.

No puedes volver a casa solo. Tu hermano debe venir contigo. ¿Cómo podéis tú y tu hermano ir a casa juntos? Eso es fácil. Simplemente ama a tu hermano. Contémplalo feliz, saludable, perfecto. Míralo como un Hijo de Dios, igual que tú. Y luego Dios, vuestro Padre, os guiará juntos de regreso al cielo.

(Ahora leed todos en voz alta)

Deposito mi fe en Dios, mi Padre.
Él me guía de vuelta a mi hogar;
nos guía a mí y a mi hermano.

Lección 47

¿Quién nos guía y nos dirige de vuelta a nuestro hogar?
¿Quién conoce nuestras necesidades y alegrías?
¿Quién nos da todo y más?
Dios lo hace.

Permite que Dios te guíe de vuelta a tu hogar. Deja que Dios te haga feliz. Deja que Dios te dé todo lo que necesitas. Lo único que debes hacer es abrir tu corazón a Su amorosa Palabra. Y la Palabra es Amor. Escucha Su mensaje. En cada cosa que pienses y hagas, escucha el Amor que está ahí. Envía ese Amor a tus hermanos y recibe de Dios las bendiciones del cielo, ahora.

(Ahora leed todos en voz alta)

¿Quién me guía y me dirige de vuelta a mi hogar?
¿Quién conoce mis necesidades y alegrías?
¿Quién me da todo y más?
Dios lo hace.

Lección 48

Somos el Hijo de Dios.
Somos Amor.
Estamos en casa, en el cielo, ahora.

¿Somos nuestros cuerpos? No, somos espíritu. ¿Son todos nuestros pensamientos, pensamientos de Dios? No, sólo los pensamientos felices y amorosos son Pensamientos de Dios. ¿Quién decide si tendremos pensamientos felices o infelices? Nosotros lo decidimos. ¿Qué eres tú realmente? Tú eres Amor, y el Amor siempre trae felicidad. ¿Dónde está tu hogar? Tu hogar está en el cielo, y el cielo está aquí y ahora. Todo lo que necesitas hacer es sentirte amoroso y feliz, y encontrarás el cielo ahora.

(Ahora leed todos en voz alta)

Somos el Hijo de Dios.
Somos Amor.
Estamos en casa, en el cielo, ahora.

Lección 49

Yo soy tal como Dios me creó.

¿Escuchaste realmente lo que acabo de decir?
"Yo soy tal como Dios me creó".

Di esto conmigo ahora:
"Yo soy tal como Dios me creó".
Piensa en lo que eso significa. Dios creó sólo Amor. Dios sólo da felicidad y alegría. Dios es tu Padre, y tú eres como tu Padre.

Di esto conmigo de nuevo:
"Yo soy tal como Dios me creó".
"Yo soy perfecto".
"Yo soy Amor".
"Yo soy el Hijo de Dios".

Lección 50

Nosotros vamos juntos al hogar de nuestro Padre.

Nuestras lecciones de todo un año están casi a punto de terminar. Hemos aprendido Quién es realmente nuestro Padre. Hemos aprendido quiénes somos realmente. Hemos aprendido que es nuestra decisión, no la de Dios, ser felices o no. Sabemos que Dios sólo da Amor. Y hemos aprendido lo más importante: 'No podemos alcanzar el hogar de nuestro Padre a menos que llevemos a nuestros hermanos con nosotros'. Muestra a cada uno de tus hermanos Amor total. Da a cada uno tu felicidad y alegría, y Dios os guiará juntos de vuelta a casa.

(Ahora leed todos en voz alta)

Nosotros vamos juntos al hogar de nuestro Padre.

Lección 51

Estoy en casa.

El cielo es el hogar de la felicidad. El cielo está lleno de paz y Amor. El cielo está dentro de tu corazón. Ahí está Dios nuestro Padre. Ahí está el mensaje que nos dará todo lo que pudiéramos desear, si tan sólo decidimos escucharlo. Hemos aprendido a escuchar y oír la palabra de Amor de Dios. Hemos aprendido a enviar Su Amor a todos nuestros hermanos. Hemos aprendido cómo estar en el cielo ahora mismo. Simplemente debemos elegir ser felices y amorosos. ¿Dónde estás tú ahora mismo?

(Ahora leed todos en voz alta)

Estoy en casa.

Lección 52

Venid, pequeños, y oiréis algo acerca de vuestro Padre del cielo: ¿Dónde está el cielo?

Ahora dejad que los niños contesten:

Simplemente en mi corazón.

¿Cómo puedes encontrar el cielo?

Simplemente debo mirar dentro de mí.

¿Cómo conocerás el cielo?

Simplemente Dios, mi Padre, me hablará.

¿Cómo oirás a tu Padre?

Simplemente aquietando todos mis pensamientos.

Y, ¿qué mensaje te enviará tu Padre?

Simplemente que yo soy parte de Él, y Él es todo.

¿Cuándo conocerás a tu Padre?

Simplemente nunca le dejé de conocer.

Epílogo

Tú y tu alumno habéis seguido un abrupto sendero en un largo viaje. Juntos habéis salido del tiempo utilizando el propio tiempo y os habéis acercado más a la conciencia de vuestra verdadera realidad.

Recuerda sólo la felicidad que este año transcurrido te ha brindado. Mira hacia atrás sólo para ver cuán lejos has llegado y date cuenta de que en el viaje que has realizado fuiste ayudado por el Único Que Conoce tus necesidades y te guió a lo largo del camino que elegiste.

Ahora tu trabajo acaba de empezar, pues ahora acabas de comenzar a sentirte vivo. Ahora acabas de empezar a ver tu verdadero papel. Ahora acabas de empezar a asumir tu verdadera función. Tú eres el salvador del mundo, y junto con tu alumno seréis salvados.

Comienza tu trabajo ahora. Pues Dios está siempre contigo, y es Su voluntad junto con la tuya la que te guiará de vuelta a tu hogar.